Actor, author, playwright and TV personality, Lee Dunne was born in Dublin in 1934. He grew up in one of Dublin's worst slums, and after a varied career as an actor, barman, clerk, dishwasher, factory-hand, ship steward, singer, truck driver and waiter which ranged all over the globe – from the USA to New Zealand and back to Ireland – he started to write while working as a London cabbie.

As well as novels, Lee Dunne has written plays for theatre, radio, TV series, such as 'Callan', 'Troubleshooters' and 'No Hiding Place', and films, often acting in them himself.

David Rawe.
Oct 1979

Also by Lee Dunne

Lee Dunne

The Day of the Cabbie

Futura Publications Limited

A Futura Book

First published in Great Britain in 1975
by Futura Publications Limited

ISBN 0 8600 7256 8

Printed in Great Britain by
Hazell Watson & Viney Ltd
Aylesbury, Bucks

Futura Publications Limited
Warner Road, London SE5

CHAPTER ONE

Bond Street stretches from Oxford Street, taking in Old Bond Street, on its way to where it forms a T-junction with Piccadilly.

As streets go, Bond is as good a mixture as you'll find, of the old and the new, the chic and the classy, the expensive and the impossible. You can get coiffed, coteuried, felt fed or phoocked, at the most expensive rates around, and if you've touched for some useless family treasure that would make a good Christmas present for the man who has everything, this is the street where you get it auctioned.

On any Friday of the year, one hundred and fifty thousand people walk up and down, and across Bond Street, sixty per cent of these being female. Which means that one hundred and eighty thousand pairs of boobs, forty per cent of them devoid of support, bounce along, nipple position varying, anglewise, from say, zero, to anywhere around ninety-five degrees. Think of that next time you're in the street on a Friday, but try hard not to get run over by a truck.

Obviously, the boobs come in all shapes and sizes, ranging from the too firm, rubbery orange shape, to the frightening proportions of drunken dirigibles, while another bundle just slap along like so much tripe with nowhere to go.

All of this may seem by the way but I mention it to illustrate how unlucky I was on that chilly day in March. It was a Friday too, so any of thousands of tasty ladies might have hailed me as I poodled the cab through the Brook Street intersection.

Instead of which, I touch for a fella who turns out to be The Paperhanger. Naturally, I didn't know this at the time or he'd never have got the chance to hang some paper on me.

He came out of Fenwicks like a fella who'd decided he wouldn't buy the store for his Missus because it wasn't classy enough. He was smiling like the old Aga Khan must have done every time his starving people got it together to give him his own body weight in diamonds, and when he ran his slender hand through his blond locks, you knew he was touching something very special. His blue eyes sparkled as he suggested I take him to Harrods, and I could almost taste the Brut which seemed to waft my way on his breath. So what, I thought, maybe the geezer likes to drink after shave.

The traffic was Friday too, if you know what I mean. Bumper to bumper, shoppers, in their innocence, looking for a place to park, not tuned in enough to know that they might as well go down to Vauxhall or Kennington to begin with, park the car there, take a bus or a cab back West, and not be causing traffic jams while they ponce about wishing for a miracle. I mean, its become so ridiculous that you feel privileged if you can find a double yellow line to park on.

By the time I'm slurping through Berkeley Square, my passenger is singing 'On With the Motley' or 'Vesta La Giba' or whatever it was that that poor clown Pagliacci was ranting and raving about, and he's not doing a bad job on it. I find myself thinking about the fella who sang for his supper, and hope my fare doesn't think he's paying me in advance. Like no way. Believe me. Not if he was Tito Gobbi himself.

As I've said before, you get plenty of time to think when you push a London cab around for a living. Even when you're barrelling along, driving fast as opposed to sitting in a traffic jam, you work automatically so that your thinking is not in any way stultified by the work you're doing.

I spent a good few years deliberately not thinking. About anything, but that kind of comfortable cocoon existence couldn't last. My head just refused to shut off like that, and I turned into an earthling. Not being able to face the reality of say each day's news, I had in the last few years turned to

6

reading nothing but escapist literature, and spending most of my time behind the wheel, either chatting up chicks, or trying to work out just what my fare did for a living.

Chatting up chicks is favourite of the two pastimes but it's expensive, even if you only consider the time you spend in the feathers as the result of your chatting up, whereas just guessing about people is harmless, cheap, and never likely to send you rushing around to St Paul's Hospital in Endell Street, Covent Garden, for a quick course of Streptomicin.

So what did my slender, elegant, obviously wealthy, passenger, do for a living. Where did he get the bread to look like he'd stepped out of *Vogue*, and how much bread must he have had to be singing baritone as I turned right into Piccadilly?

He could have been anything. Like, if you have enough of the folding stuff, you can learn how to look like class. You can do a course in how to epitomize acquired nonchalance, you can learn how to eat, drink, talk, kiss and get laid. And I guess you can be tutored to give off a vibe that makes the other guy feel privileged to be in the same room as you.

My passenger had it all, whether it was *acquired* or inherent, and he sat back on the seat as though he expected I should be looking at him in my pussy mirror. Which I was every so often. Like you can't take your eyes off the road in London for more than two seconds without hitting somebody up the chocolate.

He had a tan that could have been a lamp job. It might even have been make up except there was no way this fella was a faggot. And he was in shape, not just weightwise in relation to his six one in height, you could practically hear the muscle tone and that had to come from a lot of exercise.

The first words he said to me reached my ear as we hit Knightsbridge. His accent, which I hadn't copped when he said Harrods, was upper crust with gold inlaid. Like, you can meet those blue blood types, with and without bread. The accent, and the toffee that goes with it, the Savile Row suit, the brolly and the bowler; if they belong in the city; the short back and sides haircut, all of it can often mean nothing. You can always tell the ones who have nothing in the little brown jug by the kind of querulous quality in everything they do and say. They carp and complain, and generally behave like a drum major with a bad case of athlete's foot.

'This emporium holds little or no charm for me,' he tells me, as I pull up by the front door.

The doorman has the nearside door of the cab open in a flash but Goldilocks is still talking to me.

'But I'm trying to find a present for a lady who has everything.'

Wouldn't you know, I thought, allowing my ego a smile in homage to infallibility.

'I have a number of other calls to make and I wonder if you'd allow me to hire you. I promise you I shan't be long and you'll do jolly well out of it.'

I wasn't that interested in a long job. You could come unstuck when a fella was popping in and out of the cab, but this fella had me intrigued, so I said I'd wait, that if I wasn't there when he came out, to hang on because it meant I was mooching around the block to avoid getting a ticket or a hard time from the traffic Gestapo.

Legally you're entitled to twenty minutes to load and unload, but you try telling that to a copper or a warden, when either one or both of them has had a row with the opposite number, like the wife or the husband. No way is it worth the hassle, because the cabbie loses out too often.

I'd no problem that day and my passenger was back out in ten minutes, asking me if I'll go down the Fulham Road. I won't bore you with the details, but the number of shops and stores we hit that afternoon, with him emerging empty-handed, really had me convinced that his lady had everything.

But he bore his disappointment well, and when I dropped him at Claridges, he gave me a cheque for a tenner.

Normally I wouldn't take a cheque from the Archbishop of Canterbury, but this fella had me wrapped around his pinkie. He flashed a banker's card at me, stuck a number on the back of the cheque, and told me I was a gentleman. He was gone then into the hotel, and not only had I not come up with an answer as to where his money came from, neither had I checked the number on the kite against the number on the banker's card. That was my first mistake.

CHAPTER TWO

That cheque was interior sprung, like it had plenty of bounce, and I felt very pissed off when it landed back in my hand via two banks and the Post Office. It wasn't just the tenner. Of course I felt like a schmock, and I wanted my money, but it was the idea of that bastard stroking me after I'd lackeyed around him for a whole afternoon, that had me talking to myself in the mirror as I scraped a two-day growth off my chin.

'He's not getting away with it, no way. Flash git, giving me all that crap. You're a gentleman. . . . The lady who has everything. . . .' I cut myself twice shaving, something I rarely do, and I was so annoyed with myself for getting annoyed, that by the time I stopped myself bleeding all over the furniture, I was angry enough to have thumped my smooth-talking kite merchant right in the teeth.

Annie arrived as I was making myself some lunch and she laughed like a brass who'd just realised she had a gold mine between her thighs. Annie was my flatmate, an air hostess with Pan Am, and we had the kind of brother and sister relationship that precluded the need for bullshit like secrets from each other. So I'd told her about the cheque and about the guy who stroked me.

Annie thought I was a very shrewd character, so she got a double bang at the idea of me being turned over.

'This is my good friend Annie,' I said to the wallpaper. 'My flatmate who thinks I'm a shrewdie, laughing her knickers off because I got lumbered with a Malayan Gregory.'

'What the hell is a Malayan Gregory, Danny?' She had stopped laughing, but her dark brown eyes twinkled with interest. Annie was fascinated by any kind of slang.

'Where does all the rubber come from?'

'Malaya?' Annie didn't sound too sure, which was all right with me, because I wasn't certain myself where all the rubber came from.

'That'll do,' I said.

'All right.' Annie nodded. 'The cheque was made of rubber. But what's the Gregory bit?'

'Gregory Peck, cheque,' I said.

'I like that.' She smiled. 'Gregory Peck, cheque.' She rolled it around in her mouth.

'How was Jamaica?' I asked, as if I didn't know. You only had to look at her, dark as a half-caste, her auburn hair moving to blonde from sunshine, gentle sachets of contentment under her huge eyes, to know that Annie had got just what she'd gone for.

'Amazing, Danny. Just gets better every time I go.'

'Good for you,' I said, with meaning. 'Nice to meet a chick who knows exactly what she wants, and then goes and gets it.'

We didn't have to elaborate on that, and she got up to wash the dishes while I took a look at the newspaper. Annie was twenty-four years old, and a really good-looking chick with a spectacular body. She was into smoking pot and getting laid by black people. That was her total bag, and she preferred to do both things at the same time in the sun. So every time she was entitled to a free plane ride, she headed for the West Indies. She liked to be laid in a field of grass, and I don't mean the kind of grass cows go for, but the kind that you roll into cigarettes. I hadn't been to Jamaica but according to Annie, there were whole meadows of new smoking material all over the place. And no shortage of willing studs to keep her panties free of steam.

You might wonder how I came to be sharing a pad with such a swinging chick without trying to throw the leg myself. Well, it had happened at a good time for both of us, and we'd started out on the understanding that we could live without making love to each other.

The lease on Lautrec's pad had run out and the landlord decided that he'd be better employed hiring it out to a couple of call girls, for which you couldn't blame him. I'd been looking for a place to stay when I touched for Annie in the cab just after her flatmate had gone and killed herself.

Annie was very low that night, a bit drunk too, which wasn't her style, and I'd gone in with her for a cup of coffee, knowing that we were both talking about coffee and conversation. Not that I wouldn't have slipped her one if the vibe had been right, but I know enough about women, and I've had enough women to be aware that sometimes they need you to give them something, like your shoulder, or your ear, without you looking for anything in return.

She was cut up about her friend, a lovely young bird who just came home one night and hit the sleeping pills in the worst way. No reason that Annie knew of, nothing. Just goodnight and goodbye. So I sat there and listened to her, letting her talk, drinking her coffee, and rolling her a few joints in an attempt to put her head somewhere else.

I smoked a bit with her that night, though I could have lived without it. Hash could give me a buzz sometimes but mostly it left me cold, and I never bought it. But the odd time I did enjoy it, and there were times when I'd been glad to have some. That night with Annie, though, I smoked just to keep her company.

She was looking around for a flatmate, I mentioned that I was looking for a pad, and then she laid it on me about herself. She was hung up on black people, male or female, but I could live there with her if I picked up half the rent and what have you, and provided I didn't mind finding the odd Spade around the place, usually in the early morning.

I made her laugh then, telling her about Paddy Lautrec and Leprechaun, and the scenes we used to produce in Lautrec's flat. And when I moved in I brought Paddy's phallic symbols, and the pictures of him flashing his big muscle, and I wondered if he'd have turned Annie on to white hampton if he hadn't been in Turkey or Afghanistan or wherever the hell he was.

Anyway, that was how I came to have Annie as a flatmate, Annie of the big eyes and the long sexy legs. Annie, whose family had nothing but money, and no time for a girl who not only wanted to do her own thing but who made the mistake of telling them just what she was into. A loner, really, a bit like

12

me, so we got along really well, no rows, no petty jealousy, and no making judgements about each other's behaviour.

When Leprechaun met Annie his eyes had popped. He couldn't believe that I wasn't muff-diving or something while Annie was asleep, but then, despite being my great mate, The Lep, when it came down to sex, had no principles at all, and he was inclined to judge everybody else by his own standards. Again though, in fairness to him, when he realised that Annie wasn't about to throw a few shapes under him, he accepted her as a mate, and drove her crazy sometimes as he described in graphic detail what he'd been up to, or down to, the night before.

After lunch that day, I more or less made up my mind to forget about the bouncer. I know I'd given myself a lot of Dick Tracy type dialogue while I'd been shaving, but, what was the point? How the hell could I go about tracing a guy in a city with at least eight million people in it. My only chance was if I ran into him again, or saw him in the street. Some hopes.

Once I thought about it like that, I didn't feel so bad. It was only a tenner after all, and again, it was my own fault for being on day work. Like at night, nobody would even bother to ask you to take a cheque. Are you kidding? But I'd been trying again to get my head together about day work, feeling it was time I started working when normal people worked, and not be out and about half of the night six times a week, just to get my bread and a little nooky on the side.

About once every two years, I made a stab at day work, and like now, something happened to drive me back to nights, wishing I hadn't bothered. Nights suited me best because I was a gypsy, a wanderer who needed new experiences, new people all the time. So, I was just working myself into a grateful mood to my cheque-bouncing friend, when Leprechaun arrived and I told him what happened. That changed everything.

13

CHAPTER THREE

'Coo! Don't tell me you got caught as well.' Leprechaun shook his head and sat down in my chair by the electric fire.

'What do you mean, as well?' I said, pulling up another chair for myself.

'Haven't you heard then?' He scowled. 'No, 'course you ain't heard. You've been doin' matinees, haven't you?' He never approved of my efforts to make a go of working days.

'Well, we've got some kind of nutter on our hands. Gotta be a nutter, hasn't he? Geezer goes around bouncing kites on cab drivers.' His face was like a map of a country called experience, with dissipation like swampland tarnishing what had once been a wild, carefree sort of terrain. The eyes still had it though, imp-filled buttons that could register gnomish delight, moving into malicious mischief with one flick of the lids.

'Well, it's nice of someone to tell me about it, after I've been taken.'

'Your own bleedin' fault, innit? Poncing about on days, old dolls to Harrods for jars of bleedin' marmalade, geezers nipping into Fortnums for a tin of tuna fish, make me laugh you do, honest.'

He told me then about the kite merchant, and finally, sheepishly, admitted that he'd been taken himself. Thirty drivers, all bar five being night men, including the Lep.

'Didn't anybody put the word around?' I didn't understand how the guy had managed to stroke so many drivers. Anything out of the way, like a hard nut who lived in such an area, a brass who liked to work off the fare in the cab, or a kink who paid well, this sort of thing was passed around among the drivers as a kind of protective thing.

14

'None of 'em wanted to admit they'd been turned over,' Leprechaun said.

'Including you?'

He nodded and gave me a grin. 'Yeh, including me.' He was embarrassed, unusual for him, and I thought of the power of piss taking. Like in the cab trade if you stuck your neck out in any way, the piss-taking was cruel, and here was a situation where thirty drivers had been cheated of their money, just because one or two fellas, the first ones to be taken, hadn't dared admit to their mates that they'd come unstuck.

Something else that made me think the Lep was right when he said the kite merchant was some kind of a nut, was the fact that all the cheques were for a tenner, usually for a fare that was somewhere in the region of a fiver. So the Paperhanger wasn't doing it for the bread, which meant he had to be at it for kicks, or revenge or something like that.

'What did he look like?' I asked Leprechaun.

'Slim geezer, dark-haired with a moustache, hands like a piano player.'

I guessed he meant long slender fingers, but the dark-haired bit and the moustache threw me.

'Not the same fella,' I said. 'The guy that caught me was blond, almost golden-haired, and he had no moustache.'

'That's the funny thing, Dannyboy. Not one cabbie's given the same description of the fella, yet all the kites we've seen have the same signature. And they come out of the same kite book.'

'How did he catch you?'

'Oh, I had no chance, did I?' The Lep stood up, shaking his head like a Spaniel with the DTs.

'He got in the cab and told me he wanted a really tasty brass. Oi Oi, I thought, a handy jax coming my way. Then he tells me he wants to watch me give her one in the back of the cab, that he'll give me a tenner for my trouble. Trouble? I thought it was my birthday, didn't I? Anyway, I went looking

15

for Charlotte the Harlot, touched for her, the geezer give her seven quid for a quickie and I performed with him sitting on the dickie seat telling me what a great Hammerman I was.'

I felt sorry for my mate. Getting taken in those circumstances. I mean, like every other cabbie who liked to think he was hip, and this includes me, the Lep drove about at night praying for such a job. And from time to time a driver touched for this kind of kink, usually ending up getting well laid and well paid.

'Charlotte wouldn't have a kite. She got cash beforehand, so what could I say when the geezer told me he had no more change? Besides, that Charlotte and me, we'd really gotten it together, and I was still thinking about it when he hung the paper on me.'

I knew Leprechaun had been with Charlotte before, but I wasn't surprised he'd been spaced out by what had happened in the cab. His whole bag was group sex, and to have an audience, especially one that was paying for the chance to watch his butt move like a fiddler's elbow, well, he was just bound to flip out over that.

'I suppose we'll just have to write it off, all of us,' I said, trying to be realistic. 'Just not take any more kites ever, not from anybody.'

'Kills me to think of a geezer getting away with it. Takin' the piss out of us like that.' Leprechaun stood with his butt to the two-bar electric fire.

'I don't see what we can do. We don't even know what the face looks like, and bright though we may be, I mean, I wouldn't even know where to start.'

'What about the bank? Maybe they could tell us something about him.'

'How? If he's using a bent kite book, how would they know him?'

'Yeh, I suppose you're right.' Leprechaun sounded dis-

16

appointed, and I didn't blame him. It would have been nice to nail this character, whoever the hell he was.

Not thinking about it, I picked up the cheque again and it was then the signature hit me. Jesus! How dumb can you be? I knew that name from somewhere and up to that second it hadn't registered.

'C. F. Charming,' I said, thinking aloud.

'Yeh,' Leprechaun snorted. 'Charming, fucking Charming.'

'C. F.? You're right,' I said, 'That's what it means.'

'So what's so exciting?' The Lep was looking at me and I suddenly realised I hadn't told him what I knew.

'Do you remember that face, what was his name? Man In a Suitcase, remember him at Lautrec's one night?'

'McGill, you mean? The kite merchant with the eight different accents.'

'That's him. And eight different pen names too, one of them being this C. F. Charming.'

'You're kidding.'

'No, I'm sure of it,' I said, remembering Lautrec filling me in about the blond-haired guy with the easy smile and a hang-up on using other people's cheque books.

I'd met him at a party in Lautrec's pad though the word party is really a euphemism for what went on when Paddy Lautrec organised a happening in the pad I vacated just before I'd moved in with Annie. Lautrec was no longer with us but the memory lingered on. He'd taken off, which was something he'd always intended to do, after he and the Lep and I had had our Green Badges taken by the Public Carriage Officers for getting caught in the Jeyes Fluid, while we were having a gang bang with the Duchess Of I'd Better Not Say.

Up the Nepalese trail was all Paddy had said when I asked him where he was going. By all acounts, every junkie worth his sniff or his skin pop, had to make that trip at some time or another. I don't know whether they go in search of fresh air, new smoking material, or just to have a chat with some Guru or other. But whatever the reason, I was sorry to see Paddy go, and I still hoped that some day when I went into the cab shelter at Knightsbridge, he was going to be sitting there, a benign smile on that face of his, which one pot-walloper from St Stephen's Hospital had referred to as 'shit with muscles'.

I reminded Leprechaun about the particular party, and he started to nod his head as it all came back to him. It had been a pretty wild night, a real orgy, with a lot of laughs, which is what most orgies are best for, and I could remember McGill's face as clear as if I'd seen it the day before.

'Wonder if he still gets round the Planet in Belgravia?' the Lep said.

'There's one way to find out,' I told him, picking up my jacket on the way out.

CHAPTER FOUR

The Planet in Belgravia wasn't what it used to be. Still very much the fashionable Belgravia boozer, but lacking the lunatics of yesterday, who, just as everybody else gets older, move on, fade away, or just plain die. There were still a few of them about, real losers trying to hang on to yesterday's memories as though they were about to happen again. Bad painters who had made names for themselves as 'characters', writers who never wrote anything, and one or two professional house guests.

The pub had two big bars on two levels. Newcomers, passers-by, of which there weren't many, settled for the downstairs bar, not knowing that the upstairs room was the Holy of Holies. I remember the days when the regulars upstairs looked down their noses at innocent invaders who didn't know any better, and I'd seen many a guy thrown down the stairs simply because his face didn't fit.

It wasn't like that any more, and the old trout behind the bar gave us a smile by way of a welcome as I ordered the Lep a pint of beer and a gin and tonic for myself. Leprechaun smiled at her with such bare-faced lust that the old girl got a turn-on, and I shook my head inside, wondering how he could even think about it.

The old girl must have been sixty, but she was big, blonde and buxom, and I knew that given half a chance, the Lep would be in giving her a seeing-to amongst the empties. As I say, I marvelled at how he could fancy such an old boiler, but I knew that to him a woman was a woman, age meaning nothing, and anyway, despite the fact that he looked like a tired thirty-six-year-old, I reckoned he wasn't that far from chalking up his half century.

I took another look around as he started to chat her up. There was a familiar face in one corner of the bar, an angry-looking guy with mad eyes, but I couldn't remember his name, and when his eyes passed over me without any sign of recognition, I let it ride.

Leprechaun had the bar lady, like there was no way you could think of her as a barmaid, twitching in her roll-on by this stage, and when he bought her a large gin, I assumed she was going to get lucky later in the evening.

'Danny, meet Dorothy.' He grinned at me and I had to smile at the evil bastard. I mean, how could you not be glad to have him around? Sooner or later, he was going to be humping old Dorothy good and proper, which meant he should have been getting a fee from the Government just so he could continue spreading a little sunshine.

'Dorothy knows McGill but he hasn't been in for a while,' the Lep said.

Dorothy served me a smile and I tried to kill the image of what she'd be like with her top and bottom set in a tumbler by the bed.

'How long would you say, since you've seen him?'

She gave that some thought but her eyes drifted to the Lep's face and her bosom heaved noticeably until I repeated the question.

'Oh, six weeks, I'd say.' She threw me a fast glance, forgiving me for interrupting her indecent thoughts, and I bought her another large gin. That put me in strong with old Dorothy, which at that moment was about as useful as pneumonia, but you never knew. I sat on a stool sipping my gin and tonic, while Leprechaun started hitting her with every chord in his stack.

I didn't know what we were going to do now. It had seemed so simple, to go looking for McGill, maybe find out who was hanging all that paper under his pseudonym. But if he wasn't around, I just didn't see what else we could do.

The geezer was finished putting bouncers about anyway. Now that the Lep and I had admitted we'd been caught, and all the other faces were willing to stand up and be counted, no cabbie would accept a cheque from anybody. So why bother even looking for the guy?

There was nothing in it except aggravation, and fat chance of catching him anyway. I remembered thinking that his suntan could have been a lamp job, or even make-up. Then I'd dismissed the idea of the guy using slap because he wasn't poofy in any way. But by the sound of it, no two cabbies giving the same description of the Paperhanger, he was using make-up and whatever else it took to change his appearance. For example, the time he caught Leprechaun he had to be using a wig plus the false moustache.

It didn't make any kind of sense, a fella going to all that trouble just to ride around in cabs for nothing, and in the Lep's case, do a little piking on the house. Which reminded me again that I agreed with my mate that the face was a nutcase who got his charge by putting one over on cab drivers.

I wondered if he had been a mini driver or maybe even a small mini proprietor. What I mean is, a guy with a small fleet who'd maybe gone out of business thanks to us putting the cabfather out of business. You never could tell what would drive a guy nuts, and the Paperhanger had to be completely Brazil.

At that moment I was greeted with a slap on the back and a yell that put my jockeys into a twist. The fact that my vertebrae survived the blow heartened me slightly, and the next thing I knew, Maggie McNab had pulled my face around and was treating me to a wet one that I could have lived without.

Maggie was like a hangover with boobs, a nightmare from yesterday and better days with Lautrec. She'd been around in the early days when he lived on a diet of duck's eggs and dexedrine, and the pair of them together had turned half of Chelsea on to kinky parties, long before the suburban swop

21

scene had got under way. So while she was just another hard-drinking amoral chick now, Maggie had been in on the wild life when it first came out. Somehow she remained good-looking, her face fine and well defined, her eyes clear of the stripes her drinking and drugging had earned, and her body was still lithe despite the kind of abuse that would make a dustbin look dissipated.

When I got her tongue out of my mouth, she gave Leprechaun the same treatment, and when he pulled her off his face, she went around the bar and gave Dorothy the sexiest kiss of the three. Fair play to the old girl, she responded with a heart and a half, laughing then like an out-of-tune piano as Maggie tried to get at her boobies.

'Doesn't change much, does she?' The Lep moaned as though he was talking about the weather.

Maggie hopped back around the bar and I nodded at Dorothy to give her a drink. The old girl was definitely turned on by this time and I could see that Leprechaun had some work out ahead of him if he didn't fall into the feathers with her. You can say what you like, but an old boiler like that takes some satisfying, and don't let anybody ever tell you otherwise.

'Where did you disappear to Danny, for Christ's sake? I haven't seen you in months.'

I gave her some spoof about working to buy a place of my own, not bothering to tell her that her not seeing me was a very deliberate piece of manoeuvering on my part.

'You just disappeared out of the pad,' she informed me as though I didn't know about it. She smiled then. 'I pulled one of the chicks that moved in. Went around to see you and this tasty blonde opened the door. On the game she is, two of them sharing. Anyway, she likes girls and we had a great evening.'

I listened to some more of the same, waiting for a chance to ask her about McGill. I didn't want to jump in too quickly because Maggie had a nose for a bit of intrigue, and I didn't want to tell her what the Lep and I were about.

Two drinks and a lot of bullshit later, I asked her about him and she told me he was flopping in her place. 'Just out of Brixton, he was on remand for a couple of months and then grassed his way out of trouble, or so I think.'

That settled it. The Lep bought another drink and we began to have a jolly time. At least that was what I wanted Maggie to think, because whether she knew it or not, she and I, and Leprechaun and his Moby-boobed barmaid, were going back to her pad when the pub shut.

Maggie was all over me and I didn't shy away when she told me I was going to give her a seeing-to when she got me home. If it meant seeing McGill, I was on. Even though Maggie couldn't have turned me on, not if I was a light switch.

CHAPTER FIVE

McGill was humping Mary the Muff when we got into Maggie's basement in Redcliffe Gardens, but nobody bothered them until it was all over. Even Maggie was subdued, telling us later that she didn't mess him about, which was her normal behaviour pattern under the circumstances, because this was the first time he'd had it away since before he went into Brixton.

McGill was high on buck's fizz, if you don't mind, and while I was wondering how he managed to work the oracle between Brixton and Earls Court, he told us he'd had two days' work in a blue movie.

'They were looking for a fat man with a little prick, so I fell in lucky.'

He measured carefully the amount of fresh orange juice to each glass of champagne and he sat there naked, drinking conscientiously while Maggie took Mary the Muff away to give her a bath.

Leprechaun was dancing with Dorothy who had good legs for such an old girl, and I was hoping he'd get her into another room and start to give her one, so that I could ask McGill what about the Paperhanger. But Dorothy wanted an audience too, so they started to remove their clothes and I thought to hell with it and just asked McGill straight out.

He was immediately upset that someone had nicked one of his pseudonyms, and when he heard that the kites were being bounced on London cab drivers he was beside himself with rage.

'That is really bloody criminal,' he said, his pale eyes burning with the booze and just plain insanity. 'What sort of people are we living with at all? No principles anymore. . . .'

I described the Paperhanger as best I could but it meant nothing to McGill.

'Sounds like Jon Pertwee,' he said, still annoyed.

'Looked a lot younger, better looking too,' I said.

Next I described the Paperhanger as he'd been when he conned the Lep but that didn't help McGill either. Not that he was all that bothered whether he could help me or not. He was just pissed off that some geezer had stolen one of his pseudonyms.

He lost interest in me then and when I followed his new eyeline I saw that the Lep and Dorothy were approaching Bechers, and I didn't doubt that my mate was having the ride of his life.

I went into the kitchen and made some coffee, ignoring the giggles and the groans of pleasure that were coming from the bathroom. I smiled to myself remembering days when I'd have just torn my gear off and jumped in with them.

'Maybe you're starting to grow up,' I said to my reflection in the mirror over the kitchen sink. 'Can't be bad, like you're only thirty-six.'

McGill had walked up and was standing in the hall looking in at Maggie and Mary in the bath. He had a pot belly and a slack arse and you could tell he'd never done a day's real work in his life. Even if you ignored the sort of practised ease with which he sipped at his glass of buck's fizz.

'Go on, Maggie my girl,' he growled, obviously sexually aroused by what he was seeing. 'Beauty, beauty beauty.' He was practically hopping about on the lino tiles. 'Only woman in London who'll crash-dive without a snorkel.'

I smiled, getting the picture in one. I turned around and he looked my way.

'Do you suppose this Paperhanger is an actor by profession?'

I laughed as he said that, wondering how he could watch

Maggie and Mary the Muff in action and be thinking about a guy bouncing cheques.

'I'm glad I'm amusing you,' he yelled, throwing the glass at my head before he turned and stomped up the hall and back to his buck's fizz.

I stood there in the kitchen trying to figure it out. The Paperhanger was obviously an actor, or at least a mimic, of some talent, but I didn't see him as a professional. Actors are mostly mad all right, and those that aren't to begin with, usually end up bananas, but they don't take it out on cabbies. Drinking my coffee, I decided to drop the whole thing. McGill was my idea of a lead, and what did we have? Nothing. So I dropped the pieces of broken glass into the rubbish bin, and went back into the living room.

Leprechaun and Dorothy had changed the lyrics but the melody was still the same. He caught my eye and I could see he was offering me a share of the action. I shook my head and ignored McGill who was sitting looking at my mate and the barmaid.

When I slipped out into Redcliffe Gardens, I lit a cigarette and slipped in behind the wheel. I didn't feel much like working but as I didn't feel like doing anything else either, I thought I might as well pick up a few quid.

That's one of the good things about driving a cab in London. You can take the motor out at any time of the day or night and take money. It doesn't matter whether you start work at one o'clock lunchtime or one o'clock in the morning, there's always somebody looking for a cab.

On the corner of the Fulham Road I trapped a fare for the West End, and as he got out, a couple asked me to run them up to Finchley. It was midnight so there wasn't much traffic about and I got my foot down, trapping at Swiss Cottage on the way back a black chick who turned out to be a mate of Annie's.

She reminded me that her name was Laura which helped

me remember that she was a dancer, and I was turned on by the open way she sat behind me on the dickey seat and told me how much she liked Annie. That's my big hang-up of course, two chicks making love, the real dream being to be the meat in a two girl sandwich.

When Laura heard that Annie was back from Jamaica, she asked me to take her down to the flat I shared with Annie. She paid me when she got out and she seemed surprised I wasn't coming in. I'm not saying she was throwing an invitation my way, but I'd say the idea had crossed her mind. I let it pass me by though because what Annie and I had was good, and I didn't want to louse it up.

Not that I wouldn't have joined Laura if she'd invited me into her own pad. But even so, I doubted if my mind would have been totally on her lovely brown frame. All I could think of was the goddam Paperhanger, and the more I told myself to forget it, that there was no way I could even trace the guy, the more something in my head demanded that I find him and do something about him.

I told myself it was more of the Dick Tracy dialogue I'd given myself when I was shaving earlier. To hell with it, laugh it off, forget it, some geezer who'd lost his marbles, playing harmless games with cabbies. And he was through anyway because no cabbie was going to take a cheque from anybody. So wipe it off, let it go, stop being dramatic about it.

I kept on working for another couple of hours and then I went into the shelter by Brompton Oratory to eat something and maybe have a laugh or two.

Leprechaun was holding forth as I slid the door shut behind my back. Dolan the Canadian who'd been such a help in smashing the cabfather was laughing his head off, one really nice guy with a sense of humour that made him a great audience. The shelter was about half full and Malteser was moving in and out of the kitchen like a one-legged skater.

Leprechaun saw me clocking Malteser's quarter turn walk,

and interrupted his very funny rendition of what had happened between himself and Dorothy to yell, 'Leave her be, Danny, she's got a bad case of the Norberts tonight.'

Malteser slammed a mug of tea down in front of me, and I could see the pain in his black eyes. 'Coo,' he groaned. 'Talk about the hanging gardens of Babylon. Have me bleedin' crippled they 'ave.'

I'd never had piles but by all accounts they were an experience not to be repeated. Leprechaun, of course, dipped his oar in good when he saw that Malteser was really suffering.

'What you expect, you Maltese ponce? Think you can take it up the Khyber all the time and not touch for the Nobbys.' And he laughed like a drain.

Malteser hobbled back to the kitchen, then his head shot back out as though he'd just thought of a good line to put the Lep down. But Leprechaun was already back on the track, laying the story on eager ears, and Malteser shrugged his great Arab face at me and disappeared in among the vegetables.

I ate a steak and french fried potatoes, drank about four cups of tea, and smoked too many cigarettes. It seemed to me that the guys in the shelter were very subdued, because they just sat and listened, whereas normally the Lep's story would have been subjected to heavy interjections of filth from the four corners of the little wooden shelter. I realised then that just about every guy in there had been taken by the Paperhanger, and I thought it a lousy shame that one guy could make so many feel stupid. That was when I decided for myself, that no matter how it had to be done, we had to find some way to get our hands on the Paperhanger.

CHAPTER SIX

The Lep and myself did extra work in movies when we were asked and we got this film work through a fat woman called Agnes Bay who had a broken-down office over a litho artist's shop in Berwick Street Market.

Agnes was all right to the Lep and me because a few times in the past we'd taken her out for the evening and the pair of us had seen to her afterwards. As I walked into her office the morning after my decision to go after the Paperhanger, I wondered how I'd ever gone to bed with her. I mean, she was fat as a pig and twice as ugly, and all I could do was tell myself that such an act of charity couldn't be forgotten when they were calling the final roll.

'Danny Boy.' She lurched up from behind the desk, reminding me of an old horror picture called 'It Came From Beneath The Sea' only in this case it was from beneath the desk. I couldn't turn around and run out of the place, well, not very well, I couldn't, so I stood there and allowed her to smother me in folds of tit and arm flab, somehow giving the impression that I wasn't really being embraced to asphyxiation.

When she put me down I sank into a chair opposite her and made small talk while she admonished me and my mate for staying away so long. 'Not that I've had any work for you, my boy, but, I still have dreams of you two giving me a reading like last time.' She shuddered at remembered pleasure and I thought the desk would disintegrate. 'I was popping my cork for a week afterwards,' she assured me with a smile as simple as the mating call of a hippo who'd been locked up for five years.

'I've started one of them UGLY agencies, Danny Boy, and

29

I'm making money for the first time in years. I've even been working myself in horror jobs, and I got a hundred for a day in a real blue the other week.'

I told her I was delighted things were going so well, and then I asked her if I could look through her copies of *Spotlight*. She was curious, but I just said I was looking for a face who might be an actor and she let it go at that.

I ploughed through the photographic casting book from A to Z, taking my time, but I came up with nothing. This didn't mean that the kiteman wasn't an actor, I just didn't see anybody who looked remotely like the guy who'd bounced me for a tenner.

Agnes was busy on the phone most of the time I was in her office but she did take the phone off the hook as I got to the end of my chore, and when she flicked the catch shut on the office door, I felt that I was starring in a remake of the 'Perils of Pauline', with me in Pauline's role.

I stood up as though I hadn't noticed the manoeuvres, and then Agnes was all over me. Great, I thought, just what I need, to be eaten to death by a Barracuda in Berwick Street.

'Agnes, listen,' I said, pulling my head back.

'Going to give Agnes a seeing-to, aren't you Danny Boy?' She had me in an embrace that would have shook Steve Logan or Mick McManus but I did manage to yell in her ear that I'd touched for a visit from the Reverend John Knox.

She put me down when she heard that, her face like an old, sad, very pale Christmas pudding, giving me a kiss of commiseration on the face. 'Never mind, Danny Boy, it's a hazard we all risk. Not the big S I hope?'

I told her no and her expression softened. 'Oh well, I've had more trouble with an ingrown toe nail than I've had with the other. Week and you'll be hard as a rock.'

I staggered out into Berwick Street grateful I was such a natural liar. If I hadn't thought that one up I'd have been upstairs performing with Agnes, so you'll understand that as

I walked through the Soho afternoon, I was even glad to be inhaling diesel fumes.

Later that same afternoon I dropped into Chelsea Police Station to have a chat with Tom Davis, a copper I liked, and the only one I ever met that I'd trust, period. Tom had helped me out in a bad barney in Pimlico about two years before, and we had the odd drink and a game of darts together. I didn't see that much of him because it would be too easy to get a name as an informer and that was something I wasn't prepared to risk even though I could have done with him for a real friend.

Even leaning, practically draped across the counter, Tom was as tall as me and I'm over five ten, and he just kept nodding his big West Country head as I told him the story about the Paperhanger.

'Sounds like a screwball, Danny,' he said, making the S sound like a Z in his Somerset burr.

'How would the law go about finding him?'

Tom shook his head. 'We'd never get him on what you've told me. Not even one of them telly coppers'd nab him with that. We'd have to hope for information, that he'd try it again and slip up maybe.'

'Information from the public?' I asked.

'Aye. And we'd put a call out over cab radio circuits asking you lot if you'd seen such and such a fella, that kind of thing. But we wouldn't get far with this fella, I'm thinking.'

Tom mentioned the possibility of fingerprints being on the cheque, which helped me remember that the Paperhanger had been wearing sheer kid gloves when he'd handed it to me. I left the cheque with Tom anyway so that he could have it checked out. I didn't hold out much hope but I thought you never know, and it's not going to cost anything.

When I got home, Annie was packing her vanity case to go to work. All those hostesses jam extra panties and tights and

31

Tampax and whatever into those little weekend cases they carry the make-up around in. Annie was no exception.

The phone rang and I picked it up. It was Pan Am calling Annie and she waved at me to take the message. It was for Miss Ann Raglan, telling her that the flight was cancelled and that she was to report for duty at nine the next morning. Annie was delighted and we decided to do something together that evening. The odd time we went to a movie together, and once or twice I'd taken her to the opera which was her special love. She had trained for a few years as a ballet dancer, loved classical music, and knew the story of every opera from beginning to end.

This was a very good part of the deal of living with Annie. She talked naturally about things I'd never been able to discuss with anybody in my life before. And she was all the time encouraging me to stop reading pulp and get my head back into decent books. She knew literature and she loved to talk about it, so that at times, we sat around half the night rapping about what you might call culture, and I'd begun to discover a great hunger inside myself.

We ate in George's Pad that evening, which is just there off Sloane Square, George being such an outrageous faggy character, that you just knew he had to be asexual, getting all his charges out of running such a great little restaurant where everything was fresh, excluding George's patter.

He always called Annie Miss Raglan, but he used Danny with me simply because I'd never told him my second name. Which happens to be O'Toole O'Reilly, prefaced by the name Laurence, so you'll understand right away that I didn't run around yelling it out at the top of my voice.

'Oh Miss Raglan, and Danny, well! This is the nicest thing to happen to me today, and just look at you Miss Raglan, a vision, a perfect vision in blue.'

George was a slim guy, not tall, but I always felt he had that kind of whipcord strength you find in lightweight boxers. He was always up to the minute with the latest fashions for men, and it was nothing to go into his Pad and find that his hair was blue or green, and once even tartan. All of which came at no extra charge.

I enjoyed the food, listening to Annie, catching the odd sentence as George weaved about, speaking in his mincing baritone, drawing a barrage of laughter here and there as he went about his business. Annie enjoyed listening to him, and we were both feeling chipper as we left the restaurant to go home and chat and listen to some decent music.

I'd parked the cab in Sloane Street about thirty yards above the square, and Annie linked my arm as we walked along the footpath. I held the back door open for her, she smiled, giving me a thank you kind sir, and then I hopped in and started the diesel engine. I pulled away slowly and it was then that the bullet shattered the back window.

CHAPTER SEVEN

Miraculously, Annie was hunched in one corner of the back seat of the cab, and her sheepskin coat, tucked up around her ears against the chill of the March weather, saved her from any slivers of back window that might have come her way.

I pulled back to the kerb and I was out, opening the back door, checking that she was all right, until she yelled at me to get down just in case Wyatt Earp decided to take another shot at us. That made me drop in my tracks using the open door as cover while I scraped into the back of the cab.

'Thank Christ you're all right,' I said, hugging her to me in sheer relief.

She was more together than I was despite her recent shock. 'We'd better report it to the police, Danny,' she said as calmly as you like.

'I don't think we'll have to go to them,' I said, as I heard the bell coming down the street. 'In this part of town the fuzz get six reports if you drop a cigarette packet in the street.'

We were still hunched together in one corner of the cab when the copper from Chelsea opened the door.

'You all right, sir, madam?' Then without waiting for an answer. 'What happened to the driver?'

I told him I was the driver and he looked at me as though I shouldn't be sitting there with my arms around my passenger.

Telling him what had happened, I suddenly realised that I might have been killed, that Annie could have had her head pierced by the bullet which had demolished the back window. And I started to shake from fright as I pulled away behind the police car down to Chelsea Police Station.

Annie and I had to go through the story again and again.

First to this detective who acted like a fella looking after the store. He went away for a little while, reappearing with coffee and the news that his superior would be joining us shortly. I shrugged at Annie and she smiled my way. God, she looked gorgeous in her blue silk blouse, while her tight blue jeans had the fuzzman champing at the bit. I smiled to myself, hoping that he thought we were living together, as opposed to just sharing a flat.

The copper's name was Brown and his superior turned out to be a Detective Inspector by the name of Wilson. A tough looking forty-five-year-old with a dour expression, which never altered once as I repeated the story once more. When I finished he looked at me as though he couldn't see me very well.

'What were you doing in this station this afternoon?'

I must have reacted very surprised because he smiled a little bit and said, 'I saw you coming out as I got out of my car.'

I went into the whole rigmarole about the kites being bounced on a large number of cabbies, which didn't elicit the slightest glimmer of sympathy from Wilson. When I finished he said, 'It's just my personal opinion but I think you cabbies deserve somebody taking you for a ride, just for a change.'

'I'm not really interested in your personal opinions,' I told him.

'Don't get me wrong. I'd like to find this kite merchant for you. I'm just not keen on cab drivers as a species.'

I didn't say anything because I felt he was deliberately trying to needle me. Which to my mind meant that he didn't buy the story I'd just given him about the shot which had put paid to the back window of the cab.

'With a name like O'Toole O'Reilly, you've got to be Irish,' Wilson said, as though this particular thought gave him a bad case of heartburn.

'I was born right here in London,' I told him, enjoying myself a little bit. I could have gone on, told him that both my parents were Irish but I waited for him to ask me before I said anything. I just didn't like Detective Inspector Wilson.

'My father's dead,' I volunteered when he'd finished making notes. 'My mother, I don't know about. She went out of the flat at home one day and she never came back.'

'How long ago was this?' Wilson asked.

'When I was a boy.'

'Didn't your father go looking for her?'

I told him that my father was sick and that my mother going off like that just about finished him off.

'You didn't look for her yourself?'

I hadn't and I told him so. 'If she wanted to go she was entitled to do it.'

Wilson looked at me for a few seconds when I said that, as though he was having real trouble believing it. That's your problem, I thought, remembering the way the old man had just let himself die. Shame over my mother walking out, pity showered on him by relatives, me trying pointlessly to get him to snap out of it, despising him in the end for just letting life slip through his fingers.

'I'll want to ask you some more questions, Mister O'Reilly.' He smiled a little bit. 'Perhaps I could drop by your place tomorrow sometime?'

I said that was fine with me and left him the phone number. He was very polite, thanking Annie for her patience, and we walked out of the Police Station.

'He didn't believe a word, did he, Danny?'

I was holding the door for her once more, suddenly going cold as I wondered if the lunatic who'd shot at us earlier was about to take another go. It was ridiculous, of course, but I don't think too well when the hair is standing up on the back of my neck.

'We'll talk about it when we get home.' I shut the door and took the cab away from there as fast as I could. Sure it was stupid and crazy to think that the rifleman was following me around, but that's how I felt on the ride back to Redburn Street.

Once Annie and I were inside, I started to breathe a little easier, but she hugged me close and I realised it had just reached her in Cinemascope that she might have been lying in the morgue with her brain smashed by the bullet that was imbedded in the cab.

Wilson had organised a team to work on the cab while he'd been talking to us, but he hadn't bothered to say anything about the trajectory of the bullet, or anything else, and I hadn't asked him for any information.

'Come on,' I said. 'I'll fix some coffee and you roll us both a Jay.'

'Danny?' Annie looked up at me, still holding herself tightly to me. 'I'm scared out of my wits, but I'm even more worried that anything might happen to you.'

I grinned at her, wanting to take her lovely face in my hands and kiss her full-lipped mouth. 'Nothing's going to happen to me,' I assured her. 'You can't kill a bad thing.'

Her mouth flickered nervously. 'That's part of it, my worry, because you're one of the best people I've ever known.'

'What about rolling that Jay? Relax both of us.'

I wasn't in any way desperate to smoke a joint, but I was anxious to make Annie let go of me. She was too special, too good a mate, for me to start trying to give her one, but the way she was holding me she was making things very hard for me, in every sense of the term.

Annie plugged in the electric fire and seconds later she had Julian Bream playing as only he can, that record of his where he works wonders with Bach, and I was in the kitchen trying to make a decent pot of coffee, telling myself that what had happened was just a nasty accident, that some nut with too much booze in him, or maybe some kook on acid or something, had just taken a pot shot out of a window, fortunatel not killing anybody as he whooped it up. But somehow I couldn't make myself believe that, and I was relieved when Annie came to stand and share the joint with me.

'Nobody would want to shoot you, not deliberately,' she said, wanting very badly to believe it.

'Hardly the husband of someone I yenced in the back of the cab,' I grinned, hoping I was right, that it was that simple. Then wishing I hadn't thought of that because if I was right, if a guy was nutty enough about his old lady to go out shooting a randy cab driver, he wasn't above trying to do it again.

'I don't want anything to happen to you, Danny, nothing bad, I mean.' Annie stood there looking at me with tears sitting on her eyes. I took her in my arms, just holding on to her lovely warm spirit, trying to ignore the lovely warm body that went with it.

CHAPTER EIGHT

I'm not a difficult fella to get along with but Wilson the copper got my back up the minute he came in the flat the next day at noon. He hadn't said a word but he gave off a vibe so heavy that I knew the interview wasn't going to be pleasant. I wasn't that surprised because the Lep had told me they'd be checking out my track record and that as soon as they had the word on me, they'd be along and likely not be as nice as they had been in the station the night before.

I'd phoned the Lep at Maggie McNab's pad and when he'd finished looking after old Dorothy, he'd come over and stayed the night in the flat. What he meant by talking about my track record, was the episode with the Duchess and our involvement with Cecil Davenport, who for my money was the fourth man in the Burgess, Maclean, Kim Philby carry on. But that was only part of what Detective Inspector Wilson wanted to talk about, as I put coffee on the table and the Lep came out of the bathroom. Annie was out over the Atlantic somewhere by this time but even so, Wilson didn't give any indication that he thought the Lep and I were a couple of poofs. But then he'd done his homework well in the short time since we'd talked and he knew as much about me as you could reasonably expect him to know in just over fourteen hours.

'You and your mates, you make quite a team, wouldn't you say, Mister O'Reilly?'

I didn't like the Mister bit. When the police act formal and polite, you are, more likely than not, in for a harder time than if the chat is all easy and on Christian name terms. I mean, by that, first name terms, because if I happened to be a Jew say, it wouldn't be Christian names, would it?

'I've only got one mate, him, Inspector.' I indicated Leprechaun with a nod of my head. 'Lots of matey aquaintances, but only one friend.'

'As cab drivers go, wouldn't you agree that you two at least, are not run of the mill?'

He sipped the coffee, looked pleasantly surprised, and said how good it was to get a cup of real coffee. Meanwhile, his Detective Constable Brown was taking the pad in as though he was a camera, and I hid the smile that wanted to surface as he reacted to all of Lautrec's phallic symbols and the photos of Paddy flashing the form.

Wilson had already taken all this in but he gave no indication of it as he gave me the kind of refrigerated look I was to come to know so well in the weeks ahead.

'There are all kinds of cabbies, Inspector, and I do think that we're sort of a race apart, generally, I mean.'

'Do you mind if I restrict you to talking about yourself and Mister O'Connor?' he asked in his very reasonable voice. I looked at Leprechaun who grinned back at me, delighted with himself that he'd been right. Wilson knew his real name, which had to mean they'd been through my files at the Carriage Office that morning. Like the files on myself, Leprechaun, and Lautrec, had to be cross-referenced since we'd all been suspended for the same reason.

'What's this all about?' I asked, as if I didn't know.

Wilson regarded me like a patient man who was determined not to become annoyed with someone who was more to be pitied than laughed at.

'You could be in a lot of trouble, Mister O'Reilly,' he said pleasantly.

'That's the story of my life,' I said with a grin, which did nothing to warm Wilson up.

'It's not a funny situation,' he warned me gently. 'And I advise you not to play games, or get smart.'

'Whether you believe it or not, Inspector, I've no intention of doing either. The grin I gave you just now was nerves, that's all. I'm still shaking over what happened last night.'

'What did happen last night?' he asked, surprising me until I realised that Annie had been right coming out of the station, when she'd said he hadn't believed one word of the story I'd given him and his assistant Brown.

'I told you what happened. Just as it happened.'

'You didn't give me any idea why though.' He finished his coffee and I didn't offer him another cup.

'I don't know why somebody took a shot at the cab. Don't you think I'd tell you if I did?'

'Not necessarily. People often have very good reasons for not telling the whole story to the police.'

'I don't know what you're talking about, Inspector.'

'You and your friends, you were suspended for a time, had your licences revoked. Can you tell me why that was? Why that happened?'

'If you know we were suspended, you already know why, surely.'

'I didn't say I didn't know. I asked you to tell me why it happened.'

'Could have been one thing, or a combination of a couple of things.' I looked at Leprechaun and he shrugged in a kind of apology. The two situations I was thinking of, had both happened because he had roped Lautrec and me in, for a giggle.

'We had a gang bang with a titled raver in a hotel in Mayfair. She had us set up as evidence for her husband to divorce her. A smudge appeared at the right moment and banged off pictures of what was happening. I saw one of those pictures the day I was suspended. It was in my file at the Carriage Office. That could have been reason enough, couldn't it?'

Wilson nodded his close-cropped head. 'You mentioned a second thing,' he said.

'I know but I'm not sure I'm wise to talk about it. It in-

41

volved the Home Office and the Foreign Office, so I don't know.'

Wilson looked at Leprechaun with a hint of derision in his expression. 'You, Mister O'Connor, you became friendly with an upper crust poof by the name of Cecil Davenport. This same man defected, and you and your friends . . .' He meant me and Paddy Lautrec . . . 'you prevented his being detained by involving the police detail in a punch-up that put six of our lads into the hospital.'

I held down a smile as I remember Lautrec, stoned out of his brains, using a baseball bat to tap a few fuzzmen into temporary oblivion, while the Lep and I fought for our bloody lives in the old-fashioned way.

'You haven't mentioned Dave Oliver,' I said to Wilson.

'I don't know a Dave Oliver.'

'Well, he was the fella who used us, well he used me really, and if it hadn't been for my mates looking out for me, God knows what might have happened to me. And that's the truth.'

'What I'm really getting at, Mister O'Reilly, is the fact that you people seem to get yourselves into the most incredible situations.'

He was dead right there, of course, and for a second I wanted to tell him about Lautrec, stoned, but balancing on his head, while he shared a joint with the Duchess, who liked to be called Bicycle, who was also balancing on her head, doing her Yoga bit, before she started to bang us all to bits that night in the Mount Regal Hotel. But I didn't bother saying anything to him. He was having trouble enough believing anything I said, without me blowing his mind for him with the kind of things that only happened to me and my mates.

Wilson lit himself a cheroot, dropping the dead match into the ashtray. 'Tell me about Mister Declan O'Boyle,' he said in an offhand way.

'I don't know any Declan O'Boyle,' I replied without thinking.

Wilson looked at the Lep. 'You, Mister O'Connor? Can you tell me about Mister Declan O'Boyle?'

The Lep shrugged. 'Never heard of him, Inspector.'

Wilson smiled, his eyes flicked to Brown and back to me. 'You're a young man with a good deal of intelligence. Yet you sit there telling me a stupid lie, at the same time expecting me to believe every other word you say.'

'I don't know what you're talking about,' I said truthfully.

'There were three of you involved with the Duchess, the same three that screwed up the capture of Mister Davenport. The names were your own, that of Mister O'Connor here, and last, but by no means least, Mister Declan O'Boyle.'

I looked at Leprechaun and together we burst out laughing. 'You won't believe this either, Inspector,' I said. 'But I didn't know that was Paddy's real name.'

CHAPTER NINE

'You didn't know that was Paddy's real name.' Wilson said it as though by repeating it, he might somehow come to believe it.

'Declan?' Leprechaun snorted. 'Coo, he's going to get a hard time whenever he comes back.'

'We christened him Lautrec,' I explained to Wilson. 'He's a little fella with a beard, and he being Irish, the Paddy just happened naturally.'

'You're all Irish, all three of you,' Wilson said.

Leprechaun was indignant, genuinely so, and Wilson almost smiled as he defended his right to be called an Englishman. 'Don't class me with them human cement mixers, twenty-four-inch bottoms, short back and sides. I'm a bleedin' Cockney even if I wasn't born within the sound of Bow Bells.'

'And I've already told you I was born in Hammersmith,' I said.

'Well, your behaviour, within the confines of your job, does have a certain Celtic ring to it, wouldn't you agree?'

'If you mean that I've behaved irresponsibly the odd time, I can't argue,' I admitted, only because he knew all the answers anyway. 'But I'm an Englishman, whether you choose to accept it, or not.'

'Your friend O'Boyle, Lautrec, as you call him, he was born in Ireland.'

'That's his problem, innit, Inspector?' Leprechaun joked.

Wilson threw him a glance that would have shrivelled a lesser being. 'What do you think about these characters who've been planting bombs here in England?' he said looking directly at me.

'I think it's sad, Inspector. They can't bring their problems over here, none of the ordinary man's business.'

'Do I take it you've no sympathy with these people then, murderers, with no regard whatsoever for human life?'

'That's right,' I assured him, meaning it too. 'Ordinary people have enough troubles without being blown up over something they don't even understand.'

'And you, Mister O'Connor?'

Leprechaun looked at him for a few seconds, killed his cigarette in the ashtray, settled back in the easy chair. 'I've no time for people who kill other people. Even in the war I hated that. But this, it's murder, innit? I mean, they can call it guerilla warfare or what have you, but killing people on their way to work, geezers who have to struggle to just stay ahead of the possee, nah, it ain't right, and nothing can make it right.'

I was impressed by Leprechaun's emotion but Wilson didn't move a muscle. 'Have you ever made this kind of statement in public, Mister O'Reilly. Say, in a pub, at a party, anywhere like that?'

I shook my head. 'I keep my business to myself, Inspector. I don't go around looking for arguments or knuckle sandwiches.'

'So last night's shooting couldn't be some hothead deciding to teach you a lesson for shooting off your mouth?'

'No way, because I keep my mouth shut.' Again I nodded Leprechaun's way. 'He knows what I think, that's it.'

'Constable Tom Davis seems to think highly of you, did you know that?'

'I think Toms a good fella,' I said, 'for a copper.'

Wilson smiled at that. 'For a copper.' He nodded his head. 'You don't like policemen.'

'In our job you learn to hate the police. Just like the bastards at the Carriage Office, they have you under the thumb; they call you a spade you better start talking with a West Indian accent, or you get nicked.'

Wilson actually laughed a bit at that. 'You don't like coppers and I don't like cab drivers, but, if you're telling the truth, we have one thing in common, none of us like murderers running around our streets. By the way, have you seen a morning paper?'

I shook my head. 'Haven't been out yet.'

'I brought you one just in case.' Wilson took a paper out of his inside overcoat pocket. 'Interesting item on the bottom right hand corner of page one.'

I looked at the newspaper, found the piece he wanted me to read and I tried not to go cold as the words hit me. It said in effect that the police believed the IRA were behind the attempted murder of a London cab driver on the previous night, that the driver's name was being kept quiet for the moment as his life might still be in danger.

I looked up at Wilson and his eyes flicked through a split second's pleasure at my being so obviously disconcerted by what I'd just read.

'Who gave them that bullshit?'

Wilson shrugged. 'I often wonder where the press get half their stories. And the way they dress up a simple incident like this makes me smile.'

'I don't think it's funny,' I said. 'This could get me in trouble with the Carriage Office.'

'I did tell you earlier that you could be in serious trouble, Mister O'Reilly.'

'Whoever gave that to the press took a right liberty,' I told him, trying not to let him see that I was scared again. 'But of course, you wouldn't have any idea who might have done a thing like that.'

'I shouldn't worry too much about the Carriage Office. Unless they come to the conclusion that you're somehow mixed up with murderers.'

46

'Do me a favour, Inspector. They'll be looking for my name before the day is out, if you haven't already given it to them when you were in Lambeth Road this morning.'

His eyebrows flickered in surprise but not for long. 'How would you know I was in the Carriage Office this morning?'

'The same way that I know you gave that story to the press,' I said, letting my indignation show. 'My instincts scream at me when somebody's setting me up for something bad.'

'Your Irish heritage, Mister O'Reilly, it shows. You're over-reacting, and dressing things up, making them more colourful than they really are.'

'I'm not dressing up the fact that some prick took a pot shot at my cab last night. And if you think I over-reacted to being a target, you're bloody right. And if you're doing what I think you're doing, you're going to see me over-react like it's going out of style.'

'And here am I sitting here, hoping you're going to help me and my colleagues.'

'Get stuffed,' Leprechaun said very quietly.

Wilson reacted to that, only just checking his anger. 'I don't think there's any need to talk like that, Mister O'Connor.' He said the name as though it denoted leprosy.

'Get out of here,' Leprechaun sighed, as though he was bored with the whole business. 'I mean, who do you think you're talking to? Couple of sod busters fresh up from Cornwall or someplace. Coming in here and giving us a load of old ballocks. He ain't done nothing wrong, if he had, you wouldn't be talking to him here. And stop waving another suspension if we don't play games with you. Him and me have just about had this cabbing lark anyway.'

'If you had nothing to hide, why lie to me?' Wilson asked calmly.

'I told you, we didn't know Lautrec's real name, or if we did, we'd just forgotten it.'

47

'Empathise, Mister O'Reilly, put yourself in my place. What would you think if the situation was reversed and I told you a story like that?'

'Granted,' I admitted. 'But you'll just have to take my word for it.'

Wilson sniffed and said, 'Can you tell me anything about the whereabouts of Declan O'Boyle?'

'He's in India or Turkey, somewhere like that. He likes to smoke shit without having his collar felt for doing it.'

Wilson looked at me, like a fella coming to a big decision. 'Your friend Mister Declan O'Boyle arrived back in England about two weeks before this latest spate of bombings began. And right now, at this very minute, I'm in possession of a warrant for his arrest. I want you to help me find him.'

CHAPTER TEN

You could have knocked me over with burp and it showed so clearly that I think Wilson believed I didn't know Lautrec, or Declan O'Boyle, as he called him, was back in England.

I glanced at Leprechaun and he was equally flabbergasted. Wilson looked from one of us to the other, smiling a little bit, but retaining the chill in his eyes.

'Your friend Lautrec.' His tongue seemed to smile at the nickname. 'He is very probably in all kinds of trouble.'

'I can't believe it,' Leprechaun sighed. 'Paddy involved in anything like you're talking about.' He lit a fresh cigarette. 'Honestly, Inspector, no spoof, if you knew him, he's like a baby. All he wants is a smoke and the odd bit of sex. He doesn't do nothing, go no place, used to work the cab like he was afraid it'd break if he did too much.'

'He could have changed, don't you think?'

I didn't think so and I told this to Wilson. 'Paddy dropped out so long ago he wouldn't know how to get back in. Wouldn't want to know anyway. He started making his own little world a long time ago, and all that interested him was keeping the sun shining in that little world of his.'

'If he was in trouble, you two would want to help him?'

Wilson already knew the answer to that one, but both Leprechaun and myself left him in no doubt that we'd do anything we could for Lautrec.

'Then I suggest you try and find him,' Wilson said. 'And if you succeed, get him to give himself up. If he does that, it can only work in his favour.'

'How long's he been back then?' Leprechaun asked out of the blue.

'Best part of two months,' Wilson answered.

'Can't believe it, can you, Danny?'

'Unless he has changed as the Inspector suggested,' I said, looking right at the Lep.

He got the message, grunted and said, 'Yeh, well, I suppose it ain't totally impossible.'

I glanced at Wilson but he was giving nothing away. 'He was a mate, and a good mate now and then,' I said, still looking at Leprechaun. 'But Christ, if he's even remotely connected with this bombing business, I want nothing to do with him, and that's straight. I'm not sticking my neck out for him if he's gone completely potty.'

'Hold on now,' Leprechaun said. 'You only have his word Paddy's involved.' He indicated Wilson who didn't seem to mind the implication of what my mate had said.

'If he's been back in England best part of two months and he hasn't been in touch, that's not like the old Paddy, is it?'

Leprechaun inclined his curly blond head. 'Granted, but we don't know for sure he did come back, do we?'

'Well, I'm just saying, if he did, and he is involved, he can stay away from me.'

Wilson stood up and his assistant Brown moved like his shadow. 'I'll be in touch, Mister O'Reilly. Would you be able to stay here for a little while?' He asked the Lep.

Leprechaun nodded and Wilson said. 'Of course, since your wife left you, you're really a free agent, aren't you?'

I looked at Leprechaun but he didn't move a hair. 'Why do you want him to stay here?' I asked.

'Just in case whoever shot at you decides to try again. Mister O'Connor might come in very handy.'

'You're really trying to cheer me up, aren't you?' I said, hating the cold-eyed bastard.

'We have to consider the possibility that the gunman wasn't just trying to force you into buying a new back window. It was only a twenty-two bullet but it could have killed you. Or your young lady. In all probability it was fired from a car parked about thirty yards behind where you left your cab.'

'Which makes it sound that I was followed when Annie and I left this place.'

Wilson nodded. 'Right,' he said with another small evil smile.

'So they know where I live then.'

'Right again,' Wilson said. 'Which is why I thought it might be a good idea for Mister O'Connor to stay with you for a few days.'

'What about your lot? Couldn't some of them hang about?'

Wilson shook his head slowly. 'That would only keep them away at a time when we want them to come out of their hidey-hole.'

'Thanks a lot,' I said.

Wilson shrugged. 'The sooner you find your mate Lautrec, the sooner all of this will be over.'

'So we have to do your work for you, without the protection of the law.'

'You don't have to do anything. But, in your shoes, I'd go looking for my mate, see if I couldn't talk a little sense into him.'

'And you have no idea where he might be?'

'None,' Wilson admitted easily. 'Our informants in the Irish ghettos are drawing a blank.' He sighed. 'Or they've been badly scared, which is why I think your little friend is involved in something very political, and very very dirty.'

'You've even got narks amongst the Irish themselves?' Leprechaun sounded truly amazed.

Wilson permitted himself a real smile this time. 'We have informants in all walks of life, Mister O'Connor. If we didn't, we'd be out of business.'

'Makes you sick, dunnit?' Leprechaun looked at me. 'Imagine one Irish geezer grassing on another.'

'Spade on Spade, English on English, Irish on Irish, Paki

on Paki. There's always someone ready to peddle information in exchange for money and/or privilege.'

Wilson made his little statement as though he was reading the minutes of the local Presbyterian Church meeting, and it was all the more chilling for the lack of emotion in his voice.

'I'll leave you the newspaper,' he said, buttoning his coat. 'There might be something you want to see on telly.' He moved to the door. 'You know where to reach me urgently. If you call and I'm not in the station, the man in charge will be able to put you in touch with me. I wish you luck,' he said, going out with a spring in his step and a wave of his hand that said very clearly, 'you're going to need it.'

The front door slammed shut but Leprechaun got up and checked that neither Wilson nor Brown was lurching about in the hallway. I smiled as he came back and shut the door.

'What do you make of that?'

'I hate bleedin' fuzz, I know that much,' he said, sitting down.

'Do you suppose Paddy's really got himself involved with the IRA?'

'Dunno, do I? Little nutter, never know what he'd do for kicks.'

'I can't believe it, Lep; anybody, but not Lautrec.'

'That was a good spoof you put on for Wilson. Nearly took me by surprise.'

I grinned. 'You know me well enough to know that no matter what Lautrec got himself into, I'd be on his side.'

The Lep nodded to the electric fire, smiling a bit, his eyes retrospective.

'I've missed the little git, y'know. He really was part of our little team wasn't he?'

'One third of it,' I said, smiling at no particular frame in the kaleidoscope that was running across the back of my mind. Lautrec doing this that and the other, always making you feel that despite his built-in insanity, he was something very special.

'I almost burst out laughing when you were saying he was like a baby.' I started to chortle at the memory. 'While you were talking to that copper, Brown was clocking the pictures of Paddy holding his hampton up to the camera.'

'Maybe the fuzz bastard thought it was a baby's leg,' Leprechaun suggested, laughing for a few seconds. 'What are we going to do?' he said suddenly.

'I wish I knew,' I said, feeling very inadequate.

'Got to find him, that's for sure.'

'Right,' I agreed. 'And I only hope we have more luck touching for him than we did in collaring the Paperhanger.'

CHAPTER ELEVEN

The Lep and I had to accept that Wilson was telling the truth about Lautrec being back in England. I mean, like most policemen, he was probably a natural-born liar but there was no reason for him to spoof us about Paddy.

We agreed between us that if our kinky little mate was going to be found, it would be better for him if we were the ones to find him. That way we might be able to help him with the fuzz, or even get him out of the country again if things looked very bad for him.

So great! We were going to start trying to discover where he was and what he was doing. But how the hell do you even begin looking for someone who isn't keen to be found, in a city with over eight million people in it? I didn't know, and Leprechaun, who could have found a chick on a troopship, wasn't coming up with any bright ideas.

I remembered Tom Davis saying that the police would put out messages over our radio circuit in any situation where a cabbie might be able to help the law. And I'd been thinking of doing this about the Paperhanger until Inspector Wilson hit me with the dialogue about Lautrec. The kite merchant was now relegated to the fourth division, like him and his funny habits around cab drivers just didn't seem to matter any more.

But my big Somerset copper mate had started something rolling inside my head, and it emerged in the shape of putting adverts in a couple of newspapers. I knew that if Lautrec was around he'd be reading the *Daily Express* and the *Daily Mirror*. He liked comic cut newspapers that didn't make too many demands on his head, and he was still capable of drooling over the inevitable bird in bikini in the *Mirror*, and making mental notes about which of the high class raves in William Hickey he'd most like to lay.

I composed an advert which read 'DANNYBOY WANTS LAUTREC TO SEEK SHELTER' and Leprechaun and I drove into Fleet Street. I stalled in the cab while he organised the ad in the *Express* and then we crept up to Holborn Circus so that he could fix the ad in the *Mirror*. The idea was a real long shot because Paddy wasn't interested in adverts unless they were drawings of corsets and bras and things, but I didn't see what else we could do.

One thing surprised me more than anything else and that was the fact that Lautrec had friends in London who could, and would, hide him. In all the years we'd kicked around together, I'd never heard him mention anybody apart from myself and Leprechaun, and the various sexual acquaintances who passed through his pad as though it was Waterloo Station.

Heading back to the flat in Redburn Street, I stopped the cab and Leprechaun nipped out to buy an *Evening Standard*. I got a nasty shock when he discovered that Wilson had released a bit more of the story to the press. It was all there, even my name, and I thought, great, seeing another suspension looming up on the horizon.

'Another suspension and I'm slinging my hook for good,' I said.

'You and me both,' Leprechaun nodded. 'Time we started doing something else anyway.'

He didn't mean it and neither did I. We were London cab drivers, and anything else in the line of work would be unbearable.

'I'm not talking about work,' the Lep said, reading my mind. 'But we could find someone like Bicycle, some rich, ageing raver, keep her happy between the two of us, and live like fucking lords.'

'We'll see,' I said, trying to smile, but scared shitless about the report in the newspaper.

'That Wilson's some sweetheart, ain't he? Scumbag.' The Lep spat the word in disgust, and I didn't disagree with him.

I was angry because I was scared but I had to stay cool just to ensure that I didn't do something stupid, like putting a bunch of fives right into Mister Wilson's mouth.

'I don't see what he's getting at, do you?'

'Devious bastard, just enjoying himself. Doesn't like cabbies, remember?'

'Got to be more to it than that,' I said, unable to take the line of thought any further.

'All we can hope is that Paddy sees the ads. I mean, when he realises we know he's here in the Smoke, surely he'll get in touch.'

'I hope so. He's got nobody but us in this town, I don't care what Wilson says to the contrary. If Paddy had any other mates here, we'd have known about them long before now.'

'Where does that lead us?' the Lep asked.

'If he hasn't got anybody else in London, you mean?' He nodded, and I gave it some thought. 'If he's here, and we are the only mates he's got, the only thing I can come up with is that someone's forcing him to be here. And I can't see that, can you?'

The Lep shook his head. 'No way, not him. He's beyond scaring, and anyway, what good would he be to anybody? All he wants is scenes and drugs. He's not into anything else.'

'You don't suppose he could be mixed up with the IRA? Really, I mean?'

'The natural thing is to laugh, even at the idea.' Leprechaun shrugged. 'But even though I can't see it, with him, you never know. Such a nutter, like.'

'But him and the IRA? Holy Christ! I'm amazed to hear myself even say it.'

Leprechaun snorted. 'Inland Ravers Association. That's the only IRA he'd be in.' He laughed for a second before adding. 'At least I hope so, Danny. If he's into the other kind, he really has flipped out.'

'He'd have to have done to be into politics,' I said. I mean

Lautrec was the last person on earth to ever become any kind of political animal. He was out in space beyond that kind of thinking. But, the idea nagged at the back of my mind, people do change. And no matter how well we know somebody, how well do we really know anybody?'

'One of us is going to have to stick close to the phone at the Shelter for the next few nights.'

Leprechaun nodded in agreement. 'Take turns, a night about, split what we earn, all right?'

'That means we'll have to really go to work on the cab. No pussy, no messing about.'

He didn't like this but he agreed with a sniff of disdain. 'Seven or eight hours without chatting up one chick. Coo, that's going to be hard graft.'

I grinned at his discomfort. 'Just try hard not to let it become a habit, all right?'

'You're joking of course,' he guffawed. 'Back seat of the cab'll think I'm on holiday, and the bleedin' engine'll think I've turned sadist. Coo! Can you imagine the frustrated pussy in this town for the next week or so?'

He wasn't joking either.

I parked the cab a little way from the flat in Redburn Street, and I still had the uneasy feeling that some head case was lining up his sights for another shot at the back of my head. But I got indoors without getting killed or even wounded, and I gave myself a hard time for being so goddam dramatic. The Lep went into the kitchen to put the kettle on and I sat down to try and work things out.

This detective trick, it looks very easy when those cats do it on telly, and by all accounts there are fuzzmen who have natural ability to deduct things before other people have an idea of what's going on, and that kind of thing. But it's not my bag, I mean, I don't have any flair for being bright in that way. So I found myself sitting there, looking at the pictures of Lautrec, not knowing where to begin to look for him, feeling somehow that the one true statement Inspector Wilson had made was the one about Lautrec being in real trouble.

After a while I phoned Maggie McNab, telling her that if Lautrec got in touch with her, she was to let me know. Even if for some reason he didn't seem keen to see the Lep or me, she was to find out where I could get in contact with him. I laid it on her about the law being after him, and Maggie knew enough about Lautrec, the Lep and I, to know that we were on his side, and that anything we tried to do for him would be for his own good. I gave her my phone number which was something I had planned never to do. But, this was a real emergency.

'Don't give this number to anybody except Lautrec, understand?'

'Don't worry, Danny,' she laughed. 'But when all this is over, I'm going to phone you up in the middle of the night, and drive you crazy telling you what Mary and I are doing to each other.'

'You sadistic cow,' I said, meaning it. Maggie knew about my hang-up, how I went crazy at the idea of two chicks making it together.

'Well, if I can get you at it badly enough, maybe you'll start coming around again. Butch though I may be most of the time, I miss that hard-working Hampton of yours.'

I sat there trying to get rid of the pictures my filthy mind was printing of Maggie and Mary the Muff, who was another raver who liked all kinds of everything. I was concerned about Lautrec and I didn't want anything to get in the way. But she was turning me on just talking about it in even the most casual terms.

She laughed at the other end of the line. 'I am getting you at it, aren't I, Danny?'

'Get stuffed,' I said, smiling despite myself.

'Oh, I will, baby, before the day is out, I promise.' And she put the phone down on me and left me sitting there trying to get my priorities back in order.

CHAPTER TWELVE

The Lep worked that first night while I sat around in the Cab Shelter hoping the phone would ring and that Lautrec would be the caller. I was up and down like a jack-in-the-box for a while, but all the calls were from people looking for cabs. By about nine the phone had stopped ringing and I sat around the Shelter like a triplet who was slow to the nipple, reading a bit, chatting to Malteser who was trying to find the courage to go into hospital and have his piles seen to for once and for all.

I didn't know too many of the drivers who used the Shelter before midnight. These were the sensible drivers, guys who went to work at about five, stopped for their evening meal by about ten thirty, went back to work as the theatres were bursting, and had the cab away home by about one in the morning.

My mates and the drivers that I got along with, were all long night men, usually hitting the Shelter at about three and eating and bullshitting for an hour or two beyond that. A lot of them then went to work the early trains, while the real nuts went looking for pussy.

Leprechaun was driving his own cab while mine was in the garage having a new window fitted. My guvnor in Fulham was still trying to decide how he was going to recover the cost, but that wasn't my problem. I drove his cab, he took the larger percentage of what appeared on the meter, and he looked after the cab, including juice, oil, and all the rest of it. But I hoped he got his money back because he was one of the best fellas in the business, and always more than decent to me.

I had to spoof Malteser about why I was hanging around

and not out working the cab. I did it with a deadpan expression and sincerity dripping from my eyes.

He knew that Leprechaun and I had pulled some birds in our time, so he was inclined to believe me. In fact, the tale I told him almost spoiled his evening.

'You pox bottle, that's what you are. You and that other git, touching for rich pussy, and me in this fucking box sweating my guts out to get a living.'

'She's not as big a darling as the Lep claims,' I said quietly. 'But she throws leg brilliantly and she's loaded with bread, and generous with it.'

Malteser grimaced, pulling his great Arab face out of shape for a second.

'And I got to go home to the missus, Coo! Every time I give her one I have to kid myself it's Racquel Welsh.'

'Claudia Cardinale's a better lay,' I said. 'Not so plastic.'

He grinned, recovering his sense of humour. 'I've had her, Danny, and all in all, I prefer Racquel.'

I drank about two quarts of tea before the Lep appeared just after midnight. He looked worn and I had to laugh at the way he sank down on the seat by my side.

'Fuck me gently,' he sighed like an aching man sinking slowly into a hot bath.

'I've never worked five hours straight before, never.'

'It was supposed to be seven,' I said. 'I wasn't expecting you for at least another two hours.'

'Piss off.' He looked too tired to even smile.

'She's been working the cab has she, ah. . . .' Malteser slammed a mug of tea down in front of the Lep. 'Still, it's giving your ring a rest, innit?'

Leprechaun sipped the tea. 'How're the dinkleberries, darlin'? All right are they? Nice and juicy are they?'

Malteser looked at me. 'You must be hard up, putting him in with your mink pussy. Coo! Just look at him. Eyes like

60

pissholes in the snow. Frighten the bleedin' life out of the old girl, I should think.'

Leprechaun realised that Malteser was talking about the spoof I'd given him earlier and he picked the ball up without even having to think about it. This was something we'd had from the time I first met him in the Snake Pit down at the Public Carriage Office in Lambeth Road. This was the basement room, like a bloody dungeon, where would-be cabbies sat, sometimes for five and six hours, waiting their turn to go upstairs and do endless oral examinations as to their knowledge of London.

'That's part of her hangup innit?' the Lep said, in his most matter-of-fact voice. 'She dresses up in a gym slip, ties her hair into pigtails, and then I frighten her half to death before I rape her.' He grinned like the evil satyr that he was, really enjoying the way Malteser's great dark eyes registered regret that he wasn't part of the scene.

'What you eating?' Malteser said, conceding defeat.

'The old girl later on, but right now I'll have two eggs, over easy, and a nice helping of french fries.'

'I don't know how you do it,' I said to him when Malteser had slurped his way back to the kitchen. 'You didn't even have to wonder if I'd spoofed him about a bird.'

Leprechaun grinned again, relishing his own badness. 'Just knew you'd tell him the tale, knew he'd be like a dog with a sore cock when I got here. Evil, you are, spoofing the Maltese ponce like that.'

I didn't have to tell him there was no word from Lautrec.

'I stuck the adverts in for two days, so maybe he'll cop one of them tomorra.'

'Maybe,' I said, not feeling very hopeful. 'Supposing he doesn't.'

'Thank you, darlin',' the Lep smiled at Malteser, who had put the eggs and chips down on the narrow table top. 'I got a Spade friend wants to meet you. I was telling him about your Nobby Styles, and he told me he's been working for years as a pile driver. Quite turned him on it did. You want his number?'

Malteser shook his head gently. 'No, thanks all the same, darlin', but something you've been suckin', I wouldn't even let it near my Norberts.' He smiled at me, delighted with himself and hobbled away.

'Good thing you wear them baggy trousers innit?' Leprechaun yelled after him.

He began eating his chips then and I wondered how he could talk like that, about Malteser's complaint, and be eating within seconds. But that was the way he was. It was all so harmless to him, just fun, that he never really thought about the implications of things he talked about.

'Hope that little git sees those bleedin' adverts,' he griped, through a mouthful of food. 'Terrible to think of him being in real bother and us not being able to give him a dig out.'

'He'll get in touch,' I said. 'He's got to. . . .'

'We going back to the pad after here?' He looked up at me and I could read his mind.

'You're thinking about Maggie and Mary the Muff aren't you?' He nodded, chewing away and I grinned. 'Well, we could drop in and have a cup of coffee.'

CHAPTER THIRTEEN

I woke up at noon the next day. Somebody was leaning on the doorbell as though rigor mortis had set in, so I hobbled out to answer it. The Lep was still snoring his head off, which I could understand after the way he'd carried on in Maggie's pad until five o'clock. I hadn't taken part because my head was somewhere else, wondering what the hell kind of mess Lautrec had got himself into, scared that by the time he did surface, it might be too late to help him.

I didn't know the guy at the door but he had a friendly smile, an unkempt RAF moustache and a pair of dark and villainous eyes. He wore a purple tweed suit under a dirty soft raincoat, and a brown trilby turned up at the sides. His teeth were his own, but the colouring came from too much nicotine.

'Did I wake you up?' he asked in mock surprise, shoving his right hand out at the same moment. 'Gregory David, I'm with the *Chronicle*, and I'm rather keen to have a word. May I come in?'

He asked it as though he knew there was no way I would refuse him. His eyes smiled as he realised that he'd made me curious and he walked into the hall. 'Jolly decent of you to see me like this, much appreciated, believe me.'

I shut the door and followed him into the living room. He was looking about and you could almost hear the shutter going as he took the room in.

'What do you want?'

'Coffee would be marvellous,' he said gratefully. 'Like me to make it? A dab hand at the old coffee lark.'

'I'll make it,' I said, firmly, feeling that things had gone his way well enough. 'You're pretty smooth, I have to hand it to you,' I said, moving into the kitchen.

He moved behind as I'd thought he would. He was a guy with too much savvy to start snooping while I made the coffee. I knew it then instinctively, and in the time ahead, as I got to know him well, I came to realise that my first re-action to him had been absolutely right.

'Sorry to get you up. Obviously you work nights on the cab.'

'Not last night,' I said. 'But I was late getting to sleep.'

'Any word from your friend?'

I put the kettle on the gas stove and turned to look at him. He stood there, cool as an Eskimo's bootlaces. 'What was that?'

He smiled, showing me those monochrome teeth again. 'I saw your advert,' he said, with such certainty that I didn't bother to deny it.

'How did you know it was my advert?' I spooned coffee powder into large mugs. 'Sugar?'

'Two please, old boy, yes thanks.' He pulled out a packet of cigarettes and I took one, only because they were Balkan Sobranie.

Exhaling, after he'd held a light to my cigarette he said, 'I got a modicom of information, about you and your friend Declan O'Boyle. A few enquiries among my acquaintances in the cab trade.' He smiled. 'You and your two friends, you're pretty famous.' He stopped and pondered on that for a split second. 'Or perhaps I should say, notorious.'

'That still doesn't explain about the advert,' I said, pour-ing water into the coffee mugs.

He accepted the steaming coffee and we moved back into the living room. He sat down as though the chair was an antique and indicated cheers with the mug before sipping at the coffee.

'If they ever decide that coffee and cigarettes are suitable candidates for the dangerous drugs list, I'll have a couple of monkeys on my back.'

I sat down at the dining table and waited for him to answer my question.

'I always read the ads,' he said. 'You'd be astounded at the stories I've come up with originating in small ads. I knew you were called Danny, which if you'll pardon my effrontery is a more suitable appellation for you than Laurence, so, putting two and two together, I made a few more enquiries and discovered that you had christened your friend Lautrec, a nomenclature which seems not only apt, but heaven-sent as a substitute for Declan O'Boyle. How's that?'

I had to smile and the bastard knew he'd got me. But then he'd really known that the moment I opened the door.

'You must lay a lot of very high IQ chicks with patter like that.'

He accepted this as his due, nodding in a matter-of-fact way. 'Work on the direct approach, naturally. No circumlocution. Lot of rebuffs, as the old colonel said, but a lot of sex as well.'

'No word from Lautrec,' I said, when I finished making his day by laughing out loud.

'Pity,' he said, as though he really meant it. 'He could be in a mess of hot water.'

'Your information comes from the police,' I said rhetorically.

'As long as we accept that I didn't tell you that. You knew it for yourself, so I'm not letting anybody down by not denying it, what?'

'Have they told you just what Lautrec is supposed to have done, what they think he might be doing?'

'Hints, old boy, no definite word. They feel he's part of this bombing squad.'

'Is there any good in me telling you that Paddy just couldn't be into a scene like that?'

'I'm interested to hear why you feel so certain, old boy.'

'The fuzz haven't told you?'

He shook his head and then took his hat off. His hair was dark, running to grey and badly in need of a weekend smothered in shampoo.

'No, as I said. A morsel of information, and that reaching me at a great premium. Damn tickets for the policeman's ball. One can only hope it's not a dance but a raffle.'

'Paddy and myself and another guy, we've been mates for years. Inseparable. He is the nicest little guy you ever met. Gentle, kinky, good really. He could no more be involved in anything political than the chair you're sitting on.'

He sat there absorbing what I'd said and I went on. 'This is not bullshit, or waffle of any kind. I know Paddy, and I'd stake my life on what I've told you.'

'Speaking of your life, you've no idea why somebody took a shot at you?'

'None,' I said.

'I wondered if it might have been our own people. You caused one or two problems in the Cecil Davenport business.'

I didn't say a word because I'd gone cold at the thought. Christ! If what he was wondering about had a glimmer of sense in it, I really could end up dead.

He shook his head, dismissing the idea. 'If it was MI Shit they wouldn't play about with a twenty-two. And they wouldn't miss first time. Those boys are real experts.'

I grabbed on to that with all my mind, feeling a gentle flood of relief move through me. I started to breathe again and he laughed. 'Didn't mean to scare you, old boy, but one has to consider every possibility.'

'How did you know about Cecil Davenport?' I asked him.

'Oh, one can find out anything if one puts a little money about, or if one knows that a certain gent in the right position likes wearing ladies' underwear.'

'You mean blackmail?' I said, astonishment riding high on my voice.

'Yes, really, that's what it amount to, of course one never uses nasty words like that. But if one knows something about a chap who is in a position to find out certain things, one lets him know that one approves totally of his sexual proclivities. Then, when the conversation is all jolly kinky, one asks him a small favour.' He smiled in real satisfaction. 'I've never know it fail.'

'You're too much,' I said, meaning just that.

'I'd like to assist you in finding your friend.' He smiled at my surprise.

'For two reasons. One, I feel he is being manipulated in some way. I didn't think that when I arrived here this morning, but I believe you know him, and I'm convinced you're on the up and up.'

'What's the second reason?' I said.

'I'd like the story, exclusive.'

'But supposing there isn't a story?' I asked.

'That would be my misfortune,' he smiled. 'I should simply have to make one up.' His smile became a grin. 'One mustn't allow truth, or the lack of it, to interfere with a good story.'

'What did you have in mind? Helping out, I mean?'

'I thought we might play up the shooting. Do an interview with you. Give them plenty of the old someone-tried-to-kill-me bit.'

My expression stopped him. 'The idea disturbs you,' he said.

'You better believe it. I'm likely to get in bother with the Carriage Office as it is. I've had one bad suspension already. A story like that could finish me as a cabbie.'

'Because of the implications you mean?'

I nodded. 'Right. If someone tried to kill me, I must have done something pretty terrible. I haven't done anything wrong, but how could I hope to convince the crocodiles in

Lambeth Road that I'm not mixed up with gangsters or political head cases? I wouldn't have a prayer.'

'You would if we give you the right kind of publicity.'

'I don't get it,' I said.

'If we write it up from the angle that it was some maniac. If I state in bold black print that your personal record is without stain, they daren't suspend you. We could have a field day, the old victimization rot, why, they'd be a laughing stock.'

'You won't stroke me?'

'I give you my word as a degenerate,' Gregory David said.

'All right,' I said. 'Tell me just what you want?'

CHAPTER FOURTEEN

Gregory David wanted me to tell him exactly what had happened, which I did. He told me again he'd write the story from the nutcase angle. Like I had no idea why anybody would take a shot at me. I earned my living from my work as a London cab driver. I had no other income from any source, and I had not, nor had I ever had, any connections with any underworld figures or any organisation that might be termed subversive. Despite my Irish-sounding name, I was born and bred in London, I had no connection with Ireland other than the fact that my parents had been born there. And so on and so on.

Gregory explained that this would keep me in the clear with the Carriage Officers and the law, for the time being anyway. Meanwhile, he hoped as much as I did, that we could find Lautrec. Because if, as I claimed, Paddy was totally innocent of the charges the police wanted to bring against him, he could use all the publicity he could get. This, so Gregory assured me, would guarantee that the law wouldn't be able to stitch him up.

I bought the deal right down the line, and I was so convinced that Lautrec was in the clear that even Gregory believed in him by the time he left my pad. He smiled as he was leaving.

'I'll play up your work in films too, might get you some work. I'd like a picture of you, too. Have you any objection to that?'

I shook my head. 'If we're going to do it we might as well do it right.'

He was pleased. 'Good, Danny. How about meeting me on

the Embankment this afternoon and we'll bang off some pics there?'

I agreed to this and he left, but his body odour lingered on until I got the spray can out and emptied half of it around the living room. He was a nice guy but I'd have laid odds he didn't use water even in his whisky.

Leprechaun appeared as I was washing the coffee mugs. He looked like a Poppadum with hiccups but he was all right once he'd coughed for about fifteen minutes. I made more coffee. That Gregory fella wasn't the only one who qualified as a caffeineaholic. Christ, I couldn't begin to function until the coffee was giving me a pain in my liver.

I told the Lep about Gregory David. He was sceptical until I convinced him that the guy was a complete rogue who even stooped to blackmail to get his information. That made him okay with my mate. He could understand a fella like that, but he said he was coming with me in the afternoon. Just to take Gregory's measure for himself. I didn't argue. Whatever I had to do until this business was over and done with, hopefully, happily, I was glad to have Leprechaun along with me.

Leprechaun and Gregory liked each other, I could see that right away, and after the pictures had been taken, with me looking very serious in most of them.

'You're entitled to look serious, old boy, some rascal trying to alter the shape of your head with a bullet, what': while the Lep sat with the Thames at his back, watching a lot of nice legs carrying a lot of nice bodies east and west along the footpath.

Gregory took us to a press club after that, and during our time there, I know that Leprechaun convinced him about Lautrec being an innocent when it came to anything other than drugs and sexual perversion.

'I accept what you both have told me absolutely. Harry, give us another tincture, there's a good chap.' He spoke to the

70

barman as though he was passing him privileged Stock Market information.

Gregory drew some more smoke into his mouth, and I wondered how his teeth would look by the time he was ninety. 'Yet, I know Wilson quite well. He's a good copper, believe me. And he's convinced that Declan O'Boyle is part of this bombing squad you keep reading about in your newspapers. The fact that your friend is Irish, could, I suppose, have something to do with Wilson believing the bombers are the IRA, but he's not the kind of man to jump to conclusions. Ah! Thank you, Harry, a gentleman and a scholar.'

'We've been all through this,' I said. 'We're just repeating ourselves but I'll say it one more time. No way could Lautrec be involved in anything like that.'

Gregory nodded as though he accepted this. But he had his reservations. 'So, Danny, somehow, in my article about you, I'm going to try and make your friend feel he's put you in the shit with the law. That way, if I do my job right, we may just encourage him to come out into the open and tell us the truth.'

'Might work,' Leprechaun said. 'Like there's no way Paddy'd drop a mate in it. Not his style.'

We finished our drinks and left Gregory in Covent Garden. It was a crisp enough day, with a breeze coming down the Garden from Leicester Square, which had just a touch of Murmansk in it.

'Let's have a few sherbets while we're in town,' Leprechaun said, as though he expected me to refuse.

I felt strangely at a loose end. Disappointed, I suppose, that Lautrec hadn't responded to the advert. At a loss too, for not knowing where to go from there. I mean, Gregory David's article might work the oracle, but it was hard to not wonder where were we, if it didn't do the trick. Anyway, I said fine, so the Lep and I walked down to the Elbow in Great Newport Street.

The Elbow was a drinking club a door or two down from the Arts Theatre Club in the basement under a boutique for men. The boutique was the kind of place George Melly had in mind when he said they take your inside leg measurement even if you're only buying a tie. The Elbow was something else again.

Leprechaun had christened it Death In The Afternoon, the place being like a dungeon, but the people who ran it were so decent to their customers that it was easy to go back there. And, it was patronised by a rich team of characters: writers, actors, artistes in general, publicans, prostitutes and piss artists, the odd fuzz and more than a couple of queer clergymen. Many famous names had done their drinking there before they started making the headlines, and many of them still came back to have a drink with Annie Athens. Need I tell you Annie was a Greek?

She was an old sweetheart despite a tough line in patter, and a frightening ability to deal with drunks, dykes and deviates of all dimensions. But when Annie liked you, you were in, and you'd have to have done something really diabolical to get the elbow from the Elbow.

We were mates but there was a sliver of reservation in her appreciation of me. It was like she was always waiting for me to fit into one slot or another, and couldn't really make up her mind about me until I did. But when it came to Leprechaun, it was a case of mutual adoration, and I'm not exaggerating when I say that whatever she was doing, she dropped it like a nympho does her knickers, when he walked into the main bar.

That afternoon was no different. The moment she clapped her chestnut-coloured eyes on him, she came around the bar and threw her arms about him. She kissed him full on the mouth as she always did, and then her right hand dropped to his crotch and she moved her hand up and down as though she was weighing his prospects.

72

'Well, my darling.' She spoke like a Holloway Road Greek chewing a mouthful of Wilkinson's Sword-edge blades, and the moment he got around her, Leprechaun lurched straight back into his own brand of Cockney, so that to hear the two of them in there together, well, what can I tell you?

Most of the time, ever since we'd been in that scene with the Duchess, the Lep had been making a real effort to talk proper. This made life a lot easier for everyone, especially me. Like before, whenever we met anybody new, I had to interpret for them as we went along. Which is a real drag if you're working on a tasty bird, like it keeps interfering with whatever dialogue you happen to be laying on yourself.

'Coo, I wouldn't 'alf loike to slip you one you lovely randy bubble.'

He looked and sounded like he was being kind to a lady who was moving the wrong way agewise, like Annie Athens must have been sixty-five, but knowing him as I did, I knew he wasn't acting. He'd been there before anyway, taking her home several times after she closed the club and spending the night with her.

'Got to, dun ye? Oi mean, old girl loike that, deserves some real pork now 'n' then. An' can she perform? Coo! Teach some of these youngsters a fing or two. An' what a plater, bloimey, she was doin' deep frote when it first come aht, now you got that tasty raver doin' it in movies.'

Standing close to Annie right there in the middle of the main bar, the Lep began miming a knee trembler, a guy having it off in the upright position. Annie played along with him, gyrating her sizeable midrift with all the ease of a belly dancer with arthritis. The crowd in the bar began to hoot and yell encouraging obscenities, and I found myself getting a show from a middle-aged poof who never stopped working in television soap opera.

Meanwhile, Johnnie Harbour, one of my favourite actors and people, and a top impressionist, was giving a commentary on the carry-on in his Orson Welles voice, handing over to his Michael Mac Liammoir voice for his comments, into his Bogart, Sidney Greenstreet, Peter Lorre, John Wayne, and so on, each and every one of them having something funny and foul to say about Leprechaun and Annie Athens.

By this time Leprechaun was really worked up and I could see that given half a chance he'd be really performing with Annie, right there in the bar. Fortunately, a stroker called Barry Shanahan, the only actor I ever met who rested between parts for eighteen years, touched for the jackpot on the slot machine in the other bar. This might not seem like any kind of big deal, but it was such a rare happening, that it took precedence over even the Lep and Annie Athens.

I felt sorry for Shanahan really. He was a nice enough guy once you'd slipped him a stripe to take off and beat somebody else's ear, and getting that jackpot had become almost a lifetime's ambition. But his joy was short-lived because every punter in the bar, most of them having carried him at one time or another, had to be bought a drink, and he looked sick as the barmaid, Lily the Lip, served them up, banging the cash register drink by drink.

I got a beer out of it, trying not to laugh as Shanahan watched his winnings disappear over the bar. Lily threw her bottom lip at him in a gesture of sympathy, raised her glass containing a large gin and tonic, and promised to give him a good seeing to at some unspecified time in the not too distant future.

A bald-headed actor, Percy Z. Peters, put his arm about Shanahan's shoulders, and, taking the piss brutally, started on a long rigmarole of thanks for the drink. He and Shanahan were old mates and there had, in earlier days, been a great rivalry between them. Now Percy couldn't go wrong. His looks were right for so many movies that he hadn't stopped working in about four years, while Shanahan couldn't get a background job in a commercial.

'I'll remember this, boy,' Percy intoned like a Welsh minister who'd been given his own private jet by the local Mine Workers benevolent society. 'When I'm down in Chile on this new movie for four months at eighty a day plus, this drink is the thing that will keep me going.'

Shanahan's head was bowed as he listened to the knife being twisted between his shoulder blades, while Percy winked and leered viciously at his audience. Slowly then Shanahan's head came up and he looked at Percy with high octane hatred.

'Listen, prick,' he hissed with the kind of venom you could photograph. 'Just remember this. If you had your fuckin' hair, you'd be out of work like the rest of us.'

The audience broke up and Shanahan smiled as the various characters bought him drinks in appreciation of the remark. Even Percy had to take seconds, which he did with a lot of style, and I turned to see how the Lep was reacting. He wasn't there any more, and when I moved into the other bar to look for him, he wasn't there either. Neither was Annie Athens.

CHAPTER FIFTEEN

Assuming that my mate and Annie had crept into her private quarters for a roll in the hay, I sat down and sipped my beer. I envied the Lep his ability to concentrate on one thing at a time. Like, if he was throwing the leg with Annie you could bet he wasn't thinking about Lautrec, whereas I knew there was no way I could be bothered getting laid until the situation had sorted itself out.

I was surprised to find that I'd stopped worrying about somebody taking another shot at me. A day earlier and I'd been as tense as a working hangman's rope, the hairs stiff on the back of my neck every time I felt I was exposed. But sitting there in the Elbow, it was as though the shot had never been fired.

I thought about the other Annie. My air hostess flatmate. She was due back home today sometime and the thought gladdened me. One of the chicks chattering away at the bar counter had the same kind of hair, auburn moving to blonde, and I found myself wishing it was my flatmate. I liked that girl so much, and I hadn't any trouble admitting to myself that I'd come to need her. Which, at that moment, to me, meant that I was still scared. There was a kind of security in my relationship with Annie that I hadn't experienced before. But then there was no sexual thing between us, and though I'd say we loved one another, there was no in love bit to cope with, which made things that much easier between us.

My reverie was interrupted by the arrival of McGill as he thumped down on the bench seat beside me.

'Planning a hand shandy by the look of you,' he said, grinning, his accent allowing strains of Northern Ireland into it for the moment.

76

I had to smile. There was something about this bastard, some sort of quality, probably incorrigibility, that made him more than bearable. Remembering the first time I'd laid eyes on him, I smiled again.

'You had a different accent, mid-Atlantic I'd call it, the first time I met you.'

He pondered on that for a moment but I could see his memory was away for the afternoon.

'Half an hour later you were very English, upper crust, like you'd just cut your mouth on a saucer.'

'In my line, you have to be a man of many parts,' he said confidentially. 'Where did we meet, by the way?'

'Lautrec's pad. First time I saw you, you were pissing into a dustbin in the area outside the flat. Talking to the wall you were.'

'Out of my brains obviously.'

His voice came back to me, like a tape playing across my mind. 'I approve of fornication,' he had yelled to the wall in front of the dustbin into which he was pumping like a fire hose. 'I believe in sex, couples, schmupples, sandwiches, scenes and gang bangs . . . I'm not against anything as long as it's not in front of the children. . . . But one thing I abhor, hate and abominate, is people screwing in the bathroom when I need to strain the potatoes. . . . It's a disgrace I tell you.'

I could see him zipping himself up, about to launch into another tirade, his right fist ascending to make his point, when he turns and sees me. An instant smile inflating his angry mouth, McGill rushing two steps to begin pumping my hand. 'My dear sir.' This said in his upper crust accent. 'Well met by lamplight, what!' His apology then. 'I hope you weren't offended by my urinating in the trash can . . . but some savage wench is blowing Gabriel's horn in the bathroom. . . .'

I remember it word for word to this day, and I had to allow that you don't remember people who don't mean anything to you.

'I'm still looking for that paperhanger,' McGill confided. 'But so far the phoney bastard is staying ahead.'

'He's cool,' I said, not committing myself, realising that I hadn't thought of the kite-bouncing smoothie since I'd heard that Paddy Lautrec was back in London.

'I'd like to know how he came across that pseudonym of mine,' McGill said.

'Maybe you hung some paper on him sometime,' I suggested

McGill brightened at that. 'I most certainly hope so. He should have paid in advance for that signature.'

He was well on the way to being drunk and his memory seemed to come and go like a bookie's runner. The chick at the bar with hair like Annie's turned around casually, saw McGill and immediately threw her glass, whisky and all, at McGill. He didn't see it coming so he didn't move, but her aim wasn't the best and the glass just shattered against the wall about two feet from his head.

'You ponce,' the girl yelled moving towards us, while Lily the Lip said;

'Oh forfacks sake, don't sling the bleedin' profits about, Betty.'

Betty leaned over the table exposing the tops of her boobies which were modelled on Gore Belisha's beacons. She was a tasty enough chick but her eyes were nasty as they burned like blue laser beams at McGill.

'Have you met Sweaty Betty, Danny?'

'Where's my mink jacket, you bastard?' she asked, giving me a glance that might have lingered a bit longer if she hadn't been so pissed off with McGill.

'This lady,' McGill half turns to me, 'she's under the impression that I took a mink jacket from the orange box in which she lives. Can you imagine such a thing?'

78

'And you took three pairs of my knickers,' Betty said in the tone she'd used earlier. 'Probably wearing them right now, you kinky pig.'

'You liked me being kinky the other night. Have you had a sudden change of heart?'

He was not in any way bothered by the accusations the chick was throwing at him right and left. She looked at me again, and for a second she seemed to have a particularly bad taste in her mouth.

'Are you a friend of his?'

Her accent was Croydon, semi-detached, and with her Bunny Girl boobs she was beginning to turn me on. I shook my head slightly in answer to her question, and she seemed, right away, to regard me in a more favourable light.

'I only came in to buy a stamp,' I said.

'What about my jacket?' she asked McGill, a bit more reasonably this time.

'You were still wearing it when I crept away from between your lovely thighs, Betty. For fuck's sake stop giving me a hard time over it.' He smiled. 'It wouldn't fit me anyway.'

'Why not?' she said viciously. 'My suspenders and my stockings and my panties, they fitted you.'

Somehow I didn't laugh, and then McGill informed her that she was confusing him with somebody else.

'Not that I've anything against a taste of transvestitism,' he said in his generous fashion. 'But I'm keeping that one for my old age.'

'You'll never see old age, you ponce. Somebody's going to cut your balls off before very long.' She looked at me again and in a way I was glad she was helping me forget Lautrec for a minute. There being nothing I could do until he surfaced, I was beginning to bore myself by being so heavy about the whole scene.

'Buy me a drink, you toerag,' she said to McGill.

He smiled and stood up. 'That's more like it, girl. A little smooth talking after all that aggression. Very healthy.' He looked at my glass but didn't say anything and when he moved to the bar, the fair-haired chick called Betty sat down beside me and immediately put her left hand on my thigh.

'I've seen you before but I'm hopeless on names.'

'Mine's Danny,' I said, enjoying the warmth of her hand on my thigh.

'I fancy you, Danny,' she said it as though she was talking about my shirt.

'That's a compliment,' I assured her, relieved to find that I meant it. To hell with it, I was thinking, why not lay some pipe with her. She was a fine chick and looked like a raver.

'Would you like to give me one then?'

I shook my head and I let her face slip a shade before I grinned and said, 'But I'd love to give you two or three.'

Relief put her face back in shape and her hand moved between my thighs.

'Let's get out of here,' she said, a tremor in her voice matching the twitch in my stomach.

I was ready to do just that but I felt I should check out whether the Lep was through tumbling Annie Athens. Yet I didn't want to go into all that. I just wanted to get her out of there and work out my frustration the best way I know. McGill solved my problem by arriving with a large whisky for Betty and another beer for me. Betty took the drink and I said thanks for the beer. McGill sat down and grinned at me.

'Has she given you a pull yet?'

'Yes I have, you Irish ponce,' Betty answered for me. 'And as soon as we've drunk up we're getting out of here.'

'She's very good in the sack,' McGill told me as though she wasn't there. 'And she sweats when you're really slipping it to her. I had to put a towel between our bellies the other night. I was slipping about on her like butter in a frying pan.'

'You're not bad yourself,' Betty told him warmly. 'Better than I expected and nice to me afterwards.'

'There,' McGill said with a real smile. 'Everything's worked out very nicely, hasn't it?'

I sipped my beer, glad that nothing surprised me any more. Betty looked at me with warm eyes that were gentle too, now. 'You don't mind me sweating, do you?'

I shook my head. 'I'm into nature all the way,' I said, wishing we were out of there at that moment.

The Lep was suddenly standing over the table. He jerked his head towards the door and I could see that whatever he had in mind, he needed me right now. He moved off and I stood up, telling Betty I'd be right back. The Lep went out of the bar and up the stairs fast. I followed him wondering what the hell had happened now.

CHAPTER SIXTEEN

'Paddy's living in County Kilburn,' Leprechaun said when I caught up with him out on the street.

He kept moving along Great Newport, back towards the Garden and where we'd parked the cab. I didn't mind that, the breeze whipping in from Charing Cross Road was enough to wipe the grin off a gargoyle.

'Annie told you?'

He nodded and I could feel the excitement in him. 'Yeh. After I give her a seeing-to she starts talking about our little mate with the beard. She was in a cab coming down through the Old Country.' This was one of our names for the Irish ghetto on the Edgeware Road. 'Saw Lautrec creeping out of the tube station. Got the cabbie to do a U-turn and went back. Said he looked rough, said he was living locally, that he wasn't cabbing any more. Writing, he said, but she guessed that was a spoof. Said he was uneasy the few minutes they talked. Looking over his shoulder all the time. Told her to go schtum about running into him.'

'She didn't get any idea where he was staying?'

The Lep shook his head. 'Nah, he wasn't putting it about. But Kilburn's a start, innit?'

'So is Mayo,' I said, remembering how many streets there were in Kilburn.

'Well, let's have a bash, see how we get on, all right?'

I said fine. He was right. County Kilburn may be a big place but compared to what we'd had going for us before we descended into the Elbow that afternoon, it was the size of a postage stamp.

The cab was sitting where we'd left it in Bow Street. It was on a double yellow line but the Lep had an answer to that one too. He'd left the back seat lying against the rear bumper, a sign, even to the thickest Traffic Warden (and they're as thick as two short planks at their brightest) that the cab was broken down, and that the driver has split to try and organise a repair job as quickly as possible.

We drove away without a ticket, which gave both of us a charge, with me sitting down in the luggage space inside the near side front door. I was silent, thinking that something serious was going on. We knew now that the fuzz Wilson hadn't been spoofing about Lautrec being back in town for about two months, and the fact that he'd made no contact with the Lep or me, well, it had me wondering in the worst way.

The idea of Lautrec staying in Kilburn had an ominous ring to it as well. I mean, Irish by birth Paddy may have been, but he had no time for the Irish per se. Like he would have laughed at the idea of being mates with the kind of Paddies that lived in Kilburn. He hated the ghetto mentality in his own people, just like he felt the Jews should get out into the Gentile world more than they were inclined to do.

'You don't suppose he has flipped, do you? Gone all Republican, I mean?'

We were mooching up the Tottenham Court Road by this time, catching the tail end of the evening traffic exodus from town.

'I can't see it,' I replied, not too sure of myself any more.

'Well something must have happened to his head. Him living in Micksville, do me favours!'

'I know,' I said. 'It has me at sixes and sevens. Don't know what to think.'

'Bitta luck droppin' into the club.' He blew the hooter at somebody up front. 'Get over, you prick. Take off the hand brake, you'll be amazed what'll happen.'

'You're a hero,' I said. 'Slipping one to Annie Athens in the afternoon.'

He grinned down at me where I was hunched down on his left hand side, his ancient baby face shining like an advert eulogising the benefits of decadence.

'Sweet old cow, why wouldn't I give her one? She's so grateful these days, you feel like one of them millionaires opening a new library or something. And she still shifts hairy pie better than most chicks. That old Dorothy the other night's the same, maybe wintry in the barnet, but no shortage of spring in the khyber.'

'I was away myself when you came back that time. That blonde chick with all that boob, she gave me a straight pull. I was about to split when you reappeared.'

'Sorry about that, chief,' he smiled and I knew I didn't mind. Not now that we had some lead, however slim, to Lautrec.

'Wasn't that Man In A Suitcase sitting there with you?'

'McGill, yeh.' I smiled at the way the blond stroker had got the chick to simmer down. 'He's still trying to get his hands on the Paperhanger.'

'Some hopes,' Leprechaun sniffed. 'That geezer's okay for a giggle, but he's bother, I can tell. Annie was telling me his credit rating's getting so bad she's half afraid to take his money.'

'She really rates you old Annie.'

'Why wouldn't she, darlin'? The stick I've give her in my time.'

We rapped away about women and sex while we poodled along in the traffic, and I was laughing a lot of the time at stories I'd heard again and again. The Lep could do that to me, make me laugh at an old story simply because of the way he told it. He had an endless flair for simile, and threw in hearty helpings of hyperbole without even knowing what he was doing. And with me being a great audience he topped himself again and again with throw-away lines that a writer would have given his two left eyes for.

I noticed though, that by the time we hit Swiss Cottage that evening, he'd quietened down. This suited me because I was trying to figure out where to begin. Sure, I was grateful we had some idea of where Paddy Lautrec was likely to be, but again, when you took Kilburn out of the London context, it was a pretty sizable place.

'Just motor round for a while, fingers crossed, all right?' Leprechaun had turned into Quex Road.

'Yeh. We should be so lucky.'

'You never know. Annie Athens touched for him in the street.'

'Right,' I said. 'But she wasn't looking for him.'

I suppose we snaked and laddered in Kilburn for thirty or forty minutes before we decided to park the cab and hit a boozer or two. Not that either of us would have expected Paddy to be sitting around drinking, but he had been in London for two months without giving us a call, and that was something I'd have staked my life against, up to our visit to the Elbow and the dialogue Annie Athens had given Leprechaun.

I don't like Kilburn, in the same way that I've no time for Golders Green. Southall and Brixton turn me off as well, but I accept that people need the kind of reassurance they seem to get from pitching in with their own ethnic group, that they feel easier among people with skin the same colour as their own. I think it's sad, though, that people try to turn a certain part of their adopted country into a small slice of the land they've left. Obviously I realise that you have second and third generation Jews, Irish and West Indian, but I still wish that the first arrivals had integrated a little more, however difficult that might have been, that they'd tried harder to help the kids be English and not clung so heavily to the old traditions in a world that changes every time you blink your eyes. None of my business, of course, but that's how I feel anyway.

The ghetto bit hits you heavily when you walk into some of those Irish boozers, and you have to read carefully when you're sharing a bar with a regiment of Wimpey's Wonders or McAlpine's Brigade. One mouthful of the wrong kind of dialogue in any of those places and you'll wind up with a mouthful of granite shaped like a hand.

At the same time there's a kind of innocence about Irish pubs in London, that you just won't touch for in any other kind of hostelry. First of all they are almost totally peopled by men, and yet there's an absence of bad language and what you might call dirty talk, and though the punch-ups can be disastrous to the premises, the fighting is mostly old-fashioned, guys squaring off at each other, punching the bejeyzuz out of the opposition, and only getting down to the nitty gritty, like using tables and chairs, when the back is really to the wall.

We started that evening with a pub called the Flag, and if you had any doubt about which flag they had in mind before you went in there, you weren't left wondering for more than a couple of seconds after the door closed behind you.

The pub was one huge room with a horseshoe bar, and the walls were dotted with pictures of the Irish rebel leaders from the 1916 rebellion. There was an Irish tricolour half hidden by an old piano in one corner, and a juke box was belting out something called 'Come Down The Hillside Maggie Murphy' which made me want to vomit.

The time was moving towards eight o'clock and to judge by the state of a lot of the drinkers, they'd gone straight from work to the bar. Mostly they drank pints and as we bought a drink I was almost desperately aware that there wasn't one female in the place.

The fella who was in charge of the bar, which ran to three barmen, looked like a great rock that one day had just decided to get up and start moving around, and I made a heavy mental note never to pick a fight with him. Leprechaun glanced from this guy to me and I could see he was allowing his thoughts to run in the same vein as my own.

It was funny really, but when I ordered the drink I found myself using just a hint of brogue, a touch of my father's accent, remembered from long ago days when he still had enough life left in him to talk. Leprechaun smiled at me and said, 'Always knew you were a bleedin' Paddy deep down.'

Fair play to him, he spoke quietly enough not to be heard by the team of building workers alongside us, and I found myself wondering what it would be like to go in there with McGill, with him ranting and raving as he'd been that night at Lautrec's when he'd pissed into the dustbin. I didn't have to be an Einstein to work out what would happen to us, but I did a little arithmetic to decide how long it would have taken before both of us were carried unconscious out on to the pavement.

CHAPTER SEVENTEEN

Leprechaun found a seat in the corner furthest from the juke box which was now giving us 'I'll Take You Home Again Kathleen.' As I sat down beside him I wondered if any of the drinkers knew that this song had been written by a German in the nineteen thirties. I had this mental picture of a great Kraut with a four pint beer mug in one hand singing 'I'll Slip You One In The Kitchen Gretchen', so the song always made me smile, just as the Lep did when I sat down beside him and he said through the side of his mouth, 'Never believe the Beatles had been and gone, would you?'

'I'll bet Genesis don't do too many gigs in this part of the world.'

'Tell me this,' Leprechaun said, again through the side of his mouth. 'Would you blow that geezer behind the bar?'

This line surprised even me so naturally, I didn't make any answer. The Lep grinned like the evil bastard that he was. 'No way, right?' I nodded in agreement with him. 'Well, let's put it this way,' he went on. 'Supposing he came in the room, turned the key in the lock and said, you blow me, or you fight me. What would you do?'

'Reach for the kneepads,' I said, my face deadpan.

Leprechaun burst out laughing, causing a few heads to turn our way, and it was this helped me realise how little the drinkers seemed to be enjoying themselves. I mean compared to an ordinary English boozer where the locals went for a few pints, the Flag was like the waiting room in the morgue.

Looking around I noticed a lot of solitary men, mostly middle-aged and over, drinking quietly, looking neither left nor right, reminding me of my father. That same grey, worse than sad look, that had enveloped him like a cloak in the last years of his existence.

These men weren't bums or drop-outs or anything like that. Most of them were clean enough and fairly tidy in their dress, and I remembered my father talking about the number of men who worked away from Ireland, going home for Christmas and two weeks in the summer, living like bachelors for the rest of the year. And I thought how much better off they'd be if they had a woman somewhere close by in London, someone as lonely as they looked, with whom they could get tucked up, instead of waiting for sleep time to arrive while they sipped pints in places like the Flag.

'Lautrec'd never come into a kip like this.' Leprechaun, still using the side of his mouth like an actor playing an American gangster, interrupted my thoughts.

'I know,' I said. 'Not if he's changed his sex he wouldn't be seen dead in here.'

'And there's no way we can start asking these guys if they know him, or if they've seen him around.'

'So we might as well split.'

He nodded and I stood up leaving the beer. When we were out on the street again, I could feel that he was as sad as I was myself.

'Jesus!' he belched. 'What a way to go.'

I didn't say anything and we hardly talked during our visits to six or seven more pubs in the area. They weren't all as bad as the Flag but even the better ones, where women seemed to drink with an ease that suggested they were welcome, wouldn't have attracted Lautrec, not if the booze had been free.

By ten o'clock we were in a pub called the Watchdog. This was a decent class boozer, running to three bars including a singing lounge. The clientele was mixed, ranging from general working class in the public bar, to a much younger crowd in the singing lounge, to a kind of sickening pseudo middle class in the saloon, where a guy who appeared, say, in a commercial for soap powder, was treated like he was Sir John Gielgud.

Leprechaun was feeling as low, as defeated as I was myself. I mean so far that evening we might as well have been sitting in the Shelter taking the piss out of Malteser. For all the good we'd done, for all the success we'd had in our efforts to find Lautrec, we might as well have been stoned out of our brains out on the Nepalese trail.

It was Leprechaun who noticed that we were attracting a certain amount of attention from a trio of faces standing at one end of the bar. We were sitting with our backs to the wall a little way down from where they stood near the door, and the Lep had clocked them in the mirror.

I took my time about getting a look at them but it didn't take more than a glance for me to know that they were heavy people. Well dressed, clean shaven, but so quietly cocky that you could feel how secure they believed themselves to be. It's hard to explain how I knew they meant trouble for us. All I can tell you is that when you drive a cab around London for a living, you do develop an ability to read a situation, an ability that people in ordinary jobs don't seem to need.

Obviously some drivers get it together faster and more deeply, than others, but most London cabbies can tell at thirty yards which guy out of three will raise his brolly for a cab, which guy will tip you, and often guess accurately the amount the guy is going to put on you. This sense, developed initially to help you cope with your job, helps you in every area of your life, and it was working overtime for me as I picked up my beer and said to the Lep. 'Were they here when we came in?'

He shook his head very gently. 'Arrived a few minutes after we did.'

'We could be in trouble. They're heavy.'

His eyes were cold as he looked sideways at me. 'Don't let it spoil your beer. We might be imagining things.'

We both knew this wasn't the case. The coldness of his eyes told me that, and he knew I wouldn't mention the possibility of bother, if I couldn't actually feel it half way down the room.

'They look Irish to you?'

'Not Irish like those people in the Flag,' I answered. 'But all Paddys don't look like they were made to build motorways and nothing else.'

'Whoever they are, I hope Lautrec's not mixed up with them.' The Lep was speaking behind his beer glass again. 'One of them's carrying a shooter.'

I went cold, living again through the seconds after that shot had been fired, remembering the way I'd scraped myself into the cab, scared shitless the gunman was going to take another crack at me.

'We could creep in the other bar, get out that way,' the Lep said.

The fear in me was turning to anger, and I knew that if the situation turned nasty this would just fuel my propensity to violence. I didn't fight it, thinking that there was an excellent chance I was going to need all the violence I could muster before the Lep and I left Kilburn.

'Do you want to split?' I asked him.

He gave me a look that said I knew better, which I did. 'If they followed us in here we might as well see what they want.'

He nodded. 'Maybe they know where Paddy is.'

I envied the Lep his cool, knowing that he didn't have the butterflies that were tap-dancing in hobnailed boots all over my nerve ends. Yet, I know too, that he could launch himself into a kind of one man demolition unit, whereas I had to build up to it. He had this instant adrenalin thing, smiling like a cherub one second, milling somebody the next.

'Hold on,' he said. 'We're getting a visit.'

Sure enough, one of the trio at the bar was coming our way. A nice looking guy, a middleweight, about five ten in height, his suit well cut, and his nails freshly manicured. But his knuckles gave him away, especially the right hand. It was a solid lump, without any definition around the butt ends of his fingers. And you didn't have to be too bright to see that when those spatulate tubes were bunched together, this guy had quite a right hand with which to quieten you down.

He stopped by our table and smiled down at me. 'Hi, Danny.' He spoke with a touch of Cockney but he enunciated well enough to give his accent a neutrality that made it hard to pinpoint which part of London he belonged to.

I nodded and he spoke again. 'We should have a chat, your mate, me and my mates. Better we do it outside, all right?'

'You know where Paddy is?' I asked him. He nodded, still smiling a bit, and I said. 'In that case you're right. We should have a talk. And outside is fine.'

He nodded and went back up the bar to his mates. I looked at the Lep and he nodded. 'Let's get started,' he said, finishing his beer.

CHAPTER EIGHTEEN

It would be all too easy to be flash after the event, to tell you it didn't bother me one bit as I followed Leprechaun out of that pub to have our chat with the three faces that had followed us in there. But I'd be bullshitting, because as the door of the pub closed behind me, I was wishing like hell that the Lep and I were somewhere else. And for a flash of a second I saw myself in the sack with the chick McGill had christened Sweaty Betty, but I didn't get time to give her one or anything like that because by this time we had reached the corner of the quiet residential street where the three faces were waiting to talk to us.

And it was quiet, even though the boozer was only twenty yards back. The Lep and I were side by side, him cool as a polar bear's ballbag, me nervous enough to be dangerous if I got lucky.

It's hard to know who had the advantage as we reached our friends. They knew what was going to happen, whereas we could only guess. But then we knew they were heavy and they didn't know a thing about the way Leprechaun could throw shapes in a tight corner. And I had a kind of advantage because basically I look like the guy you get to hold your jacket.

The funny thing is I didn't consider the fact that one of them had a shooter, because I couldn't see any of them using one in that situation.

'You wanted to have a chat you said.' Leprechaun broke the ice and the fella who'd talked to us in the bar nodded his head. He was still smiling.

'We don't want you in this manor looking for Paddy

O'Boyle.' This came from the hardest looking member of the trio in an accent which he obviously thought sounded Irish.

'You can save that ballocks,' Leprechaun said. 'That accent never come out of Ireland.'

'Your mate said you knew where Paddy was,' I said.

'None of your concern.' The tough-looking one glanced at the smiler. 'You should've put that bullet in his head.'

The smiler shrugged, somehow suggesting that he would next time. It was too much for me, and again that telepathy thing that the Lep and I shared was working, because as I punched smiler right on the button, Leprechaun had already floored the other speaker.

Smiler went out into the street and he stayed there, and I got a blow on my right temple that sent me crashing back against a wall eight feet behind me. My head was spinning until I hit the wall but the pain on contact hurled me on to my toes and I blade-kicked the fella as he moved in to clobber me again.

He was hard, that's for sure, because that kick should have had him bending over nursing his kneecap. The kick didn't stop him, but it slowed him down, by which time my left foot was in his crown jewels. That stopped him and I'd say it didn't do his fifteen jewel lever movement one bit of good. I raked his face, my right hand like a claw, following on with an inward elbow that took his head left, by which time my elbow was moving outward again, hammering the side of his face just once as he hurled sideways from the force of the blow.

As I looked around I saw the Lep kicking his man for the last time, then I was aware of the smiler getting up off the street. As I moved towards him, my mate moved past me, hauling him to his feet as though he was a bag of straw.

'Which is your motor?' I heard him ask as he pulled the smiler, who wasn't smiling any more, in on to the footpath.

'Get stuffed.' The fella's words choked off on the words,

almost doubling over, and I saw that the Lep had rammed something into his guts.

He jerked the fella up straight again. 'Which motor?'

'That one, the Rover.' Smiler gagged, and Leprechaun threw him against the side of the car.

'Keys?'

Smiler fumbled at his pocket. Leprechaun just ripped the pocket off the jacket and threw the keys to me. 'Drive around while I talk to this fella.'

He pushed the guy into the back seat and I thought Jesus Christ, as I saw that Leprechaun had a gun. I took the car away like a rocket, got my head together and slowed down before I killed all of us, or got myself arrested for dangerous driving.

'Where's our mate Paddy?' There was silence for a few seconds followed by a gasp fuelled by pain. 'Mark me,' the Lep said so quietly that it was frightening. 'I'm not playing games. Where's our mate?'

'Over a shop in West End Lane. My place, I live there.'

'Alone?' I saw the fella nod 'yes' in the rearview mirror and I was already heading north, knowing that any shops in West End Lane were at the top end.

'Right son, you tell us exactly where when we get there. And mark me well, any hanky panky and you'll lose, no matter who else wins. All right?'

'You got a driving licence?' I heard Leprechaun say after a minute.

I saw the fella reach inside his jacket, moving very gingerly, and then he handed his driving licence to the Lep.

'His name's Arthur Brians, Danny.' He put the licence into his own pocket and I saw Brians think about objecting, change his mind and go schtum.

'There,' he said. 'Over that dress shop.'

I stopped the car. 'You stay here,' Leprechaun said. 'Keep her ticking over while I get Paddy.'

He went in with Brians and I sat there wondering what in the name of Christ we'd gotten ourselves into this time. These people weren't kidding about. No fella who carried a gun was doing it for the exercise, and I knew that if the Lep wasn't so handy, and I hadn't been very lucky, the pair of us would have been left with broken legs and swollen scrotums by this time.

One thing that was clear was that they weren't IRA or any other kind of idealist group. No way. These cats were common thugs who did whatever they did for money, and not for anything as ridiculous as a cause. I smiled when I thought of that, because as much as I demand the right to be called an Englishman, I guess there's enough goddam Guinness in my blood to make me want to believe that the Irish wouldn't breed scum like Brians and his mates.

·Ridiculous, I know. As far back as you care to go the Irish have produced their fair share of scumbags, just like any other race of people.

I marvelled at the cool of guys like that Brians. Imagine taking a shot at another human being and not being bothered about the consequences. Like, if he'd killed me instead of just demolishing the back window of the cab, or if he'd killed lovely Annie, you could tell it wouldn't have kept Brians awake for one minute.

I had trouble getting that one together. How anybody could kill someone else and just get on with their business, well, it made my mind boggle. Yet, I knew London was full of people who would do anything for money, or from fear, but I honestly believed I'd kill myself before I'd cold bloodedly murder another human being.

Yet again, my reaction to finding out that Arthur Brians had been the guy to fire the shot at my cab, punching him the way I had, I'd been trying to drive my fist through his chin and up and out through the back of his head. And if he'd gone out into the road as some fella was driving by like a maniac, he could have been killed. And I knew that this wouldn't have bothered me all that much. Not at that moment anyway, but I couldn't kid myself that I'd have been able to forget it afterwards.

The door alongside the dress shop opened and the Lep came out, pushing Brians ahead of him. Brians wasn't smiling now either, and I wondered what was going through his head. Did he think we were going to kill him? And if he did, was he as scared as I'd been when the bullet had smacked through the back window of the cab? At a guess he was scared. Like he was just a fella who happened to be hard, but like the rest of us, he didn't stand up too well under real pain.

Leprechaun opened the back door of the car and threw Brians in on the seat.

'Get out of here,' he said, slamming the door. I caught his eye in the rear view mirror and he answered the question I hadn't asked. 'Paddy's not there.'

CHAPTER NINETEEN

Using the roundabout, I drove back down West End Lane, wondering where we went from here.

'Pick up the cab,' Leprechaun said. 'Leave this behind.'

'What about him?' I asked.

'He's coming with us, aint' you, Arfer boy?' The Lep was going all Cockney on me again, but at least it made me smile. Arfer boy didn't say anything, but you could tell he was wishing he was somewhere else.

'What's the score? How come Paddy wasn't there?'

'These faces had him tied up, locked in, the lot. He undid the ropes somehow, picked the lock and split. Christ knows where he is by this time.'

I turned into Quex Road and pulled the Rover over behind the cab. I stayed in the car, wiping the steering wheel clean, rubbing the door handles that Leprechaun had used, leaving the keys in the ignition, thinking it would be all to the good if someone nicked the car.

Leprechaun shoved Brians into the back of the cab and I took the keys from him through the offside rear window. I looked at him and he knew I was asking where to?

'Chelsea nick,' he said, giving Brians a tap with the gun on the edge of his rib cage. Arthur had asked for this by over reacting to the mention of the police station.

'You move like that again, Arfer boy, and I'm going to bust your rib box, mark me now, I ain't playing games.'

I started the diesel engine, switched on the lights and took the cab away. I didn't bother with any fancy cab route, just taking the motor down Edgware Road to Marble Arch, down Park Lane, around Hyde Park Corner, through my Belgravias, stopping right outside Chelsea Police Station.

'Go in, see if Wilson's there. If he's not, tell them to get him. Nothing more, all right?'

I nodded and walked into the station. The uniform in charge listened to my request and my name, and went to the phone. I didn't hear what he said, but in about a minute, Detective Inspector Wilson came out to meet me. I nodded that I wanted him outside and he followed me out of the building.

I didn't say anything because I still didn't like Wilson very much. He watched me open the back door of the cab, and I saw him react surprised when he saw the Lep and Brians.

'Well, well, long time no see, Arthur,' he said pleasantly.

Leprechaun handed Wilson the gun, handle first. 'Took this from one of Arthur's mates.'

'He's potty,' Arthur said. 'Bringing me here, bleedin' kidnapping, that's what it is.'

'Come inside,' Wilson said as though he hadn't heard Arthur. 'We'll get this sorted out.'

We told Wilson our side of the story then Arthur told his tale. He was in a boozer having a beer and we conned him into going outside. He didn't know what was happening and we clobbered him and brought him to the nick.

Wilson looked at him. He sniffed and rubbed the side of his nose with one finger. 'You surprise me, Arthur, a story like that.'

'It's gospel, Inspector,' Arthur pleaded. 'Never saw these nutters before.'

'You'll find my prints all over his drum,' Leprechaun said calmly. Then he grinned at Arthur. 'I made sure, just in case you turned turtle.'

Wilson nodded, and I could see he appreciated that. 'You know and I know, Arthur, that you haven't the bottle to go for a packet of fags without one of your mates in tow. So stop flannelling me. Won't take long to produce mug shots of your known associates.' He stood up. 'You could be in a lot of trouble, son, and you know enough about the law to realise it.'

Arthur looked like he was going to protest but Wilson stopped him. 'No more cobblers, Arthur. Just sit and have a think. I'm prepared to believe these men that you admitted pulling the trigger the other night. Porridge for that and you know it. If they're right that you had Declan O'Boyle in your drum, he'd have left some dabs about getting out of there. You should be able to work out how many charges we can get out of that one. So you sit and think, and I'll come back and talk to you in a while.'

'I'm saying nothing,' Arthur said. I felt this was more for the benefit of myself and Leprechaun. Wilson smiled, not impressed.

'Well, have a think about it. No rush.' He smiled coldly. 'I work here, remember.'

The uniformed man in the room opened the door for us and my last impression of Arthur sitting there was that of a fella trying to work out how he could get himself off the hook.

'This doesn't mean that your pal O'Boyle is in the clear,' Wilson said.

I nodded. 'I didn't think it would. But maybe when Arthur coughs he'll tell you why Lautrec was a prisoner. That could help him, couldn't it?'

Wilson shrugged. 'Might do, lad, but no guarantees.'

'I'd like you both here about eleven in the morning. Arthur should have had a change of heart by then, but I'll have some pictures for you to look at just in case. And we'll take full statements from you both.'

I nodded and tried not to look amazed when Wilson held out his hand.

'Maybe all cabbies aren't as bad as I had them painted.'

He shook hands with Leprechaun and my mate said, 'You're all right, Inspector.'

Wilson nodded his head. 'For a copper.'

Leprechaun laughed and we left him standing in the door of the police station.

I got in behind the wheel with the Lep sitting on the dicky seat behind me.

'That Wilson's coming round all right, in he?'

'So he should,' I said, meaning it. 'With you and me doing his job for him.'

'Where the fuck's Paddy gotten himself to, that's what I'd like to know.'

I smiled to myself, looking ahead so that he couldn't see it. Not that he'd have seen it anyway. It's pretty dark inside a cab at that time of night.

'Fair play to him getting out of that flat.'

'Probably smelt some rare pussy going by in the street,' Leprechaun laughed. 'That'd give him enough strength to get out of anything.'

'I don't think that's what happened,' I said, suppressing the need to laugh.

'Hope he shows up soon. I left your number with Annie Athens in case he got in touch there. And Maggie McNab'll be on like a flash if he gets to her.'

'That's if Mary the Muff doesn't get her hands on his hampton.'

'Yeh, he'd probably fancy her. Doesn't do a thing for me. Reminds me of a nosebag with tits.'

'You've got some balls criticising her. After Dorothy from the Planet and then Annie Athens. Do me favours!'

'No good telling you, is it? Them old dolls are great in the sack. Give you so much you have to work like a bastard to handle it all.'

'One thing I liked about Lautrec.' I grinned to myself. 'He wouldn't have touched old boilers like that.'

'Leave off,' Leprechaun snorted. 'That little git'd fling one up a bus. He's had anything I've had, I can tell you. He blocked Annie Athens years ago.'

'Ah yeh,' I said. 'But that was before she had to start wearing surgical stockings to keep her legs up.'

'That's a turn on in itself. You wait. You wait till I organise you with old Annie. She'll blow your mind.'

'I'd go bent first,' I said, wanting to laugh.

'Go bent as well,' the Lep said. 'Never be stuck for something to do then.'

I pulled up in Redburn Street, and Leprechaun got out of the cab. I turned off the ignition, pulled out the handle under the dash to cut the engine.

'Open the luggage door will you, Lep?'

He shrugged and opened the door, and I watched his face light up under the glow from the street light as he saw Lautrec bunched up like a ball down to the left of where I was sitting behind the wheel.

'Well, fack me gently,' Leprechaun said, emotion crowding his voice.

'Gimme a chance to get a drink or two first will you,' Lautrec said, his hairy face splitting like a coconut as the Lep reached down to haul him up out of the luggage compartment.

CHAPTER TWENTY

Lautrec looked very rough but it didn't stop all three of us hugging each other like schoolgirls who'd won a relay race, and I don't think I'm speaking just for myself when I say that all the laughing covered up a hell of a heap of emotion.

Then Leprechaun started in on me, calling me all the pox bottles that ever lived rolled into one, while Lautrec chortled in his evil way over the way we'd concealed his presence from Leprechaun on the ride down from Quex Road, and then later from the police station.

'How'd he come to be in the droshki anyway, little prick?'

'Listen to who's calling you a little prick,' I said, laughing, waiting then like the Lep while Paddy answered the question.

Lautrec was sitting down, no longer wandering about touching his phallic symbols, examining the pictures of himself in the Jeyes Fluid, like a fella who'd made up his mind he'd never expected to see them again.

He was pale and his eyes were like ulcers on an ironing board, and even his beard, longer than I'd ever seen it, seemed to be devoid of life. But his spirit was still warm, and there was need to look for the spunk that was so much a part of him.

'When I broke out of that drum, I crept down West End Lane like a snake against a wall. Quex Road was so much part of a cotton run from the days on the knowledge that I just automatically used it to get me out to Kilburn High Road.'

He paused, savouring the moment when he'd discovered the Lep's cab, his eyes brightening a bit and not looking quite so diseased.

'Can you imagine? After all this time, seeing your motor.

I couldn't believe my eyes, and then I thought maybe you'd changed over, then I thought fuck it, I'm getting in anyway. It was a place to hide in case those faces came after me.'

'You saw him the minute you got in the cab?' The Lep directed this question at me. I nodded and he shook his head. 'And me threatening to shoot that Arthur if he didn't tell me where Lautrec was.'

'You didn't expect me to say anything, did you?'

Leprechaun shook his head. 'No, something could have gone wrong. You did right, but after the nick, that was a bit strong.'

'That was for giggles,' I said, already laughing again at Lautrec.

'Great pad you have here,' he said.

'What's it all about, anyway, Paddy?' the Lep was curious.

Lautrec shrugged. 'I don't know.'

He shrugged again at our obvious disbelief. 'I woke up in that place and they kept me there. That's all I can tell you.'

Leprechaun and I shared another look. We were both puzzled, and that's putting it mildly.

'You must have some idea.'

'I met a geezer on the boat over from Europe. He had a chick with him that turned me on. And he was into scenes. They both told me that. So I went home with them, Swiss Cottage, and we got a good scene going with this chick and a couple of others that came in the pad. I was having a ball.'

'Thanks for giving us a shout like,' the Lep said, sounding properly disgusted at missing a scene, and much more like his old self.

'I would have done. This geezer was all right, but before I got around to it, I must have passed out one night. I woke up in that room you saw in West End Lane, and I was stuck there till I got out tonight.'

Leprechaun looked at me and I knew he was remembering that Annie Athens had met Lautrec some time after he got back, and that he had told her he was living in County Kilburn. But I left it to the Lep and he let that one go.

'We thought maybe you'd gone Republican, joined the IRA or something.'

Lautrec didn't even bother to answer that. He smiled. 'I'd just like to know who knocked me out, what they gave me to do it, and what they wanted with me.'

'They never said nothing to you, why they was keeping you locked up?'

'Nothing.' Lautrec sounded very convincing. 'They told me if I behaved myself I wouldn't get hurt, and one night they even brought me in a spade chick for a few hours.'

'You know the law's looking for you?'

Lautrec looked as though this was news to him. 'What for?' he said. 'All I did was go to a long running party.'

'They seem to think you're connected with some of these bombings we've been suffering. You do know about them?'

'I haven't seen a paper, heard a radio, in weeks. I don't even know what day it is.'

Again Leprechaun looked at me, and I could see that however much he wanted to believe our old mate, he was having a hard time doing it.

'And you don't know what they wanted with you?'

'Listen, wouldn't I tell you if I knew? I've never had any secrets from you pair.'

'That's what we thought,' I said.

Lautrec responded to the doubt in my voice by shrugging helplessly. 'I'm sorry if you don't think so right now, but I'm telling you all I know.'

'Listen, Paddy.' Leprechaun stood up and stood facing Lautrec. 'We just left a copper, geezer called Wilson, and he wants you. He says you're connected with this bombing that's been going on. It's not us sayin' it but a Detective Inspector who's no schmock. Now're you still sayin' you know nothing?'

'I don't suppose there's any shit in this place?' Lautrec didn't sound too hopeful. 'I'm pretty strung out.'

I got up and went into Annie's bedroom. She had some hash wrapped in tinfoil in her dressing gown pocket. I walked back into the living room and sat down again. Lautrec watched me as I rolled him a joint that was wild enough to blow even his mind.

'We don't give a fack what you've done. If you have done something.' The Lep was pleading with Lautrec as obliquely as he knew how. 'But this geezer Wilson ain't kidding. And if you are in bother, we thought maybe we could get you to Ireland or something.' He grinned. 'Maybe even send you back up the Nepalese trail.'

Lautrec shook his head gently. 'I've had that scene, and I'd be lost over there in Ireland. Been away too long.'

'And you're still saying you've never been near any of those bombings?'

Lautrec looked up at the Lep. 'Can you see me planting bombs? I wouldn't plant a fucking daffodil, do leave off, Lep.'

I passed the joint to Paddy and we left him alone while he wolfed it into himself. He offered it to me but I shook my head and he went back to killing it on his own. I wondered if he'd meant what he said about the heavier drug scene. And I hoped that his experiences abroad had cured him of his liking for stuff other than pot. Like I didn't want to see him killing himself.

He seemed less frazzled by the time he squashed the butt of the joint in the ashtray. Leprechaun picked up the dog end and I heard him flushing it down the lavatory pan. He came back into the living room and Lautrec smiled.

'You're getting very careful in your old age,' he said with a smile.

Leprechaun looked at him and I could see he was close to being angry.

'Paddy, I don't know if you've got the message, but someone took a potshot at Danny here the other night. He could have been killed, seriously hurt. His flatmate, Annie, was with him, she could have been cut to bits with flying glass. Now I don't find any of it funny, and with Wilson dropping in here when it suits him, I don't think it'd be smart for him to find joint butts in the ashtray.'

Lautrec nodded by way of apology and he looked at me with gratitude in his eyes. 'I'm glad they didn't hurt you, Head, you know that.'

I nodded. 'Sure, but I have to be honest with you. I think you're involved in some way just like Wilson says.' He looked like he was going to speak but I held up my hand. 'No, hang on, listen. I'm not preaching. Like the Lep, I don't care what you might have done, but I think you owe it to us to let us in on it.'

Lautrec took this in, and I felt bad to be giving him the boot when he was suffering. But he had to be told. 'Wilson definitely gave the impression he could lay any number of charges at your feet. And I don't think he's bullshitting.'

'I couldn't hurt a fly, you both know that. Jesus!' Lautrec stood up like a man in pain. 'But there's nothing I can tell you, straight.'

'That's not the same thing as saying you don't know anything, is it?' I said.

Lautrec smiled his touché smile. 'You're too bright, Danny.'

'Is someone leaning on you?' Leprechaun asked right out of the blue.

'Like it's going out of style,' Lautrec said, sinking into the chair again.

CHAPTER TWENTY-ONE

Lautrec began talking after I'd made a pot of real coffee and rolled him another joint. The earlier one, which would have had an elephant doing a soft shoe shuffle, just about reached him. But then his tolerance to all kinds of drugs had always been phenomenal, so I wasn't that surprised. He talked about his travels, which were only important because he had found something inside himself that proved to him that he didn't want to switch off, drop out, completely.

'I need to work, to keep in touch with reality. I saw too many cats blowing their minds, young people dying from O.D's, others gone right round the twist from too many trips, the lot. And I knew it wasn't for me.'

He finished the latest J and this time he went and flushed it down the loo. When he came back he smiled at the Lep and said. 'Give me time, Head.'

Leprechaun coughed and blew his nose and I looked the other way. To have sat and listened to Lautrec, to hear him talk about virtually coming back from the dead, well, nobody's so tough that they wouldn't be touched by that.

'Touching for this fella on the boat back here, well, I thought, what harm? The chick was unbelievable, a blonde with form that belonged in the centre spread of Playboy, and I wanted to give her a seeing-to so badly, that I made her hot for me.' He smiled. 'I'm still in demand as a novelty, great, innit?'

'She must have seen the length of your Robert Young,' the Lep said, and Paddy unleashed his lengthy tongue which was like a strip of pink sandpaper. He fingered his beard then, still grinning and said. "Course, you know what happens when the brush meets the brillo pad, sparks flying. The blonde ended up with blisters on her thighs.'

'Shat ap,' the Lep pleaded, going all Cockney again. 'You're gettin' me at it, you little pox bottle.'

'Anyway, it was a good scene for a few days, her and the other chicks I told you about.'

'What about the fella? What was his scene?' I asked.

'Piker,' Lautrec said. 'Didn't perform, just clocked the action.'

'Like Wheelchair Willie,' Leprechaun said, referring to a guy in Mayfair, who paid cabbies very well to perform with prostitutes, the brass playing the virgin and the cabbie the big bad rapist.

'When I woke up in that room, the face came to see me. And the way those heavies gave him three bags full, he was the boss. He gave me details, names, times, you name it, about a girl I got in the club. Few years back. Nice kid. I fixed a plumbing job for her with an old midwife in Chiswick. The chick died but I managed to stay out of it. He had enough on me, had me bang to rights, everything he needed to get me a lot of porridge.'

'I'd just love to get my hands on him. He wouldn't do any piking for a long time,' the Lep said quietly.

'I don't know what he's into,' Lautrec went on. 'But he laid it on me about being IRA. That he was commanding a team here in the Smoke, and that they needed me on the spot a few times.' He shrugged an apology. 'I wasn't stuck in that room all the time.'

I nodded and Leprechaun told him that we'd talked to Annie Athens, and about her meeting him in Kilburn.

Lautrec looked at Leprechaun and grinned. 'Might have known you'd be in to give her a lick.' He shrugged again. 'And with the way she fancies you, she was bound to mention meeting me. Never mind, you're getting the true bill now.'

'I didn't buy the IRA bit, no way. These cats are something else though I can't say what. I had no choice, had to do what they said. Didn't seem to matter much. They were going to plant the bombs anyway. I'd nothing to do with that end of it.'

'You must have known they were setting you up,' I said.

'What could I do? Maybe there was a chance I wouldn't get nobbled. The other way I was guaranteed. If Cornwall, that's his code name or so he said, if he gave the gen about the abortion to the fuzz, I was gone anyway.'

'So you were at the scene just before some of the bombs went off?'

He nodded at me by way of answering. 'Sure. But you can believe I didn't flash my cock or anything, like, I wasn't trying to attract attention.'

'You must have been seen once, maybe more, for Wilson to be so sure it was you. He must have had a detailed description, and then got some information from somewhere.'

Leprechaun gave me a glance of appreciation. 'Ever thought of being a bogey, Dannyboy?'

'Like I've thought of being a brain surgeon.' I looked at Lautrec. 'Go on.'

'I got pissed off last week and I said I was splitting.' He shrugged. 'Me and my big mouth. They started tying me up when they weren't about. Geezer called Arthur whacked me about a bit. I couldn't handle him.'

The Lep grinned. 'Danny handled him lovely earlier on tonight. Knocked him cold with a right hand, a gem.'

Lautrec smiled and put his thumb up. 'Thanks, me old darlin'.'

I grinned, self-conscious, but very glad I'd hit that Arthur the way I had.

'We gave him to Wilson, but then you know that you muff-diving git. You were there like a soft suitcase.'

'They're heavy people,' Lautrec said. 'How come you found Arthur?'

110

'They found us,' I told him. 'We were all over the County looking for you, not knowing where to start, hoping something would break. That Arthur and two others came in the Watchdog and asked us out for a chat.'

'They're called Billy and Freddy. Hard boiled eggs both of 'em,' Paddy said.

'They didn't look too hard when we left them. He took a shooter off one of them.'

Lautrec looked worried. 'It won't stop here. I mean, just because Arthur's in the nick. He's just a muscle.'

'What won't stop here?' I asked him quickly.

Lautrec looked at me before he spoke and I was disappointed. Deep down inside me, something was ringing like a warning bell. Something wasn't quite right. I didn't know what it was but it had to mean that Lautrec was holding out. His story was good, convincing enough, but there was something missing.

'I don't know what they're after, what the aim is, Danny, and that's gospel.'

'And you know nothing about the face in charge – Cornwall, was it?'

'Nothing. He came and went, and he was all right to me till I started getting pissed off about being in that flat all the time. Then he told the other faces to do whatever they had to, to keep me quiet. And I'm not being dramatic when I say that this fella would have you killed and not blink an eye.'

'What're we going to do with him?' the Lep was asking me.

'He can stay here,' I said. 'Once we keep him out of the way when Wilson shows up.'

'What about Annie?'

'She'll be all right. Due back today or tomorrow. No sweat there. Any mate of mine is welcome.'

'Is she tasty?' Lautrec leered at me.

'Sensational,' I said. 'Into her own scene, but as you say, your novelty value is high, so you never know.'

111

I was speaking easily but I hoped that Annie wouldn't fancy Lautrec. She meant more to me than I cared to think about, and though the fact that she might throw some leg for Paddy wouldn't alter my feelings for her, I felt it would just drive a bigger wedge between us, from her point of view.

Leprechaun stood up. 'I'm going to work.'

'Look after yourself,' I said, needlessly.

'I'll be all right. Those faces won't be so flash after what we did to 'em tonight.'

He said see you, to Lautrec and I walked out to the cab with him.

'What do you think?' he asked, jerking his head towards the flat.

'Something's not right,' I said. 'He's holding out in some way.'

'Just what I thought.' He shrugged. 'Still, he may talk a bit more in the next day or two.'

'You'll come back here when you wind up tonight?' He nodded and I told him I'd leave the key under the mat outside the door. I watched him pull away and I went down the steps to the flat. I smiled as I shut the door, thinking that after all our threats we hadn't taken the piss out of Lautrec about his real name. Still, hopefully we'd have plenty of time for that when things got sorted out.

CHAPTER TWENTY-TWO

Lautrec needed to just get stoned that first night and after what he'd been through with Arthur and those other faces, I didn't try to stop him. That was his way of unwinding and it was a lot less harmful than the hard stuff, which he'd been into before he'd left England. As well as which, I didn't think he was going to do any more talking about the situation, not for the moment anyway.

He needed to rap about the good times we'd had over the years, remembering with an uncanny memory for detail, kinky scenes he'd organised in his old pad. I let him wallow in the comfort of memory, glad that he had something with which to insulate himself from the heaviness of the present. He went on and on, stoned enough not to see that I wasn't really listening that carefully.

I played some Oscar Peterson records, hoping the music would put his head into a better place. He'd always been a jazz buff, and though I'd have preferred Deep Purple or Genesis, I played what I thought he'd like to hear. But, it didn't stop him rabbiting on, and this gave me the impression that he was a lot more scared that he was prepared to admit.

This had to mean that something big was happening or about to happen. Like despite being a little guy, Lautrec had never really been scared of anything in his life. He was quiet and gentle, bent on enjoying a peaceful, trouble-free sort of life, but in a crunch, he was like one of those Irish Kerry Blue terriers. I'd seen him stand up to guys who could have chewed him up between two slices of bread, and I'd never been aware of a sliver of fear in him. But now he was double scared, and it showed enough to have me wondering what in hell we were involved in.

It was always possible that he'd found some kind of new respect for himself, which would have accounted for a shift in his attitudes to dangerous situations, but I didn't think it was this that coloured his thinking. I knew him too well to believe that, and yet, because he was still spoofing, I had to ask myself how well did I know him? Like the day before and I would have sworn on a stack of Bibles that Lautrec wouldn't hold out on Leprechaun and me.

He was keeping things back, of this I was sure, and I had to believe that his reasons were so strong that in time he'd be justified for doing things the way he saw fit. If I let go of that, if I came to the conclusion that he was just conning me, then I'd have to get up and walk away from him, leave him to Wilson or the other faces. And I knew I couldn't do that, no way, so you'll understand that he had to get the benefit of the doubt, for the time being at any rate.

At about four he fell asleep and I lifted him out of the chair and laid him down on the couch. He was a feather-weight, sleeping like a well-behaved baby, and I wrapped him in a travelling rug and left him to wander with Morpheus. Then I got into bed and slept myself.

The alarm blasted me awake at ten o'clock and I showered while the coffee was brewing. Leprechaun appeared looking like a slack snare drum, but he was in good form after only four hours' sleep, and we drank coffee together in the kitchen.

'Sooner we get this caper over the better I'm goin' to like it.' He held the coffee mug cupped in his hands. 'Again last night, a right raver hitting my ear with dialogue that had the steering wheel sweating, and I had to take a rain check.'

I smiled, pleased with him for sticking to our arrangement, that we didn't spend time pulling chicks on the cab until we got ourselves and Lautrec out of the shit. It was hard for Leprechaun because he was a guy who lived so that his hampton could have fun. We were all into chicks, but with him it was more than a pastime, sex being the generator of his every action. And all the pussy he touched for came off the cab, like he never went to pubs or clubs or whatever, to make time with chicks. The cab was his social life base as well as the means by which he earned his living, so he was a bit crippled by the restrictions of our arrangement.

'You're a hero,' I said automatically, not intending to take the piss.

'Fackin' right,' he moaned, gulping down the hot coffee. 'This chick had ideas that even I hadn't thought of.'

'Such as?' I didn't really care because I was wondering what sort of reception we were going to get from Inspector Wilson at eleven, but he needed to tell me and it was no hardship to listen.

'She wanted to confess her sins to me. Me playing the priest, her telling me the story, and what dialogue. Coo, I never heard anything like it. Then I had to give her penance, like the Catholics do, y'know, all sexy stuff, no prayers nothing like that.'

The idea turned me on, I have to admit, and I could sympathise with the heavy percentage of chagrin in my mate's expression.

'You got her phone number?' He nodded you better believe it, and I said, 'Why not go see her tonight. It's my turn to work the cab. Have a night away from all this. You can tell me all about it tomorrow.'

He shrugged. 'I don't know. Seeing Paddy, knowing he's giving us some spoof, be a shame to waste a chick like that. She deserves your whole head, wouldn't you say?'

I had to agree with him. A raver like that couldn't be taken casually. I mean you didn't touch for that kind of scene every day in the week, so it had to be given all your attention.

'I thought he might have coughed some more last night but it didn't happen. He's afraid of something, really afraid.'

115

'He's changed then,' the Lep said, and I nodded. 'He was never afraid of nothing, you know it.'

'I was thinking, maybe with getting off the hard stuff, maybe he thinks life is more important now. That would account for him being scared.'

Leprechaun didn't buy this. 'If they threatened to shoot him, say, I think he'd laugh in their faces. I mean, he may have changed a little, but he's still the same potty little bastard. And anyone telling him what to do? Christ, they really must have something big on him.'

'You don't buy the abortion story then?'

'Course not.' Leprechaun's voice was like a sniff of the nostrils. 'Load of ballocks, that, but I thought, let him get on with it. Can't force him.'

'If we accept that he is telling us the tale, and we admit he has changed, you don't think he could have changed enough to be covering up for some of that IRA team in London?'

'I don't know, Danny. He's potty enough to get involved for a cause. I wouldn't have said that yesterday but listening to him last night, well, right now, I wouldn't put money on him laughing at the idea. He would have done one time, but now I just don't know.'

'You don't suppose he's likely to split while we're with Wilson?'

Obviously this hadn't occurred to Leprechaun. 'Why? Why would he take off?'

'I don't know,' I said. 'Just wondering that's all.'

'He came to us, like when he found the cab he climbed right in there. I can't see him going back out there. Faces probably looking for him, and he'd be on his own.'

'I'm sure you're right. Anyway, he'll probably sleep the clock around.'

The Lep nodded. 'So if we creep out quietly, take the phone off the hook, he won't be disturbed.'

'Remind me to ask him later where that fella, the boss,

where he lives in Swiss Cottage. Like to take a look at that geezer.' Leprechaun was holding the door for me when the thought hit him, and I made a mental note not to forget it.

The sun was shining as we pulled the door softly behind us, locking Paddy in, hoping he'd be safe and sound till we got back. It was cold, March still holding the cards, and I shivered as I climbed into the luggage area beside the Lep who was doing the driving.

I kept my eyes open for any sign of Arthur's mates from the Watchdog. If they wanted Lautrec back they might well be hanging around waiting for him to be left alone. I didn't see anybody that bothered me, but then how the hell would I see anybody who didn't want to be seen?

We got to the nick without incident. The Lep parked the cab and we walked in together to see Wilson. He was waiting for us and he seemed to nod his approval that we had got there dead on eleven o'clock.

'Come on in, men,' he said in a friendly way. 'I have some pictures I'd like you to look at.'

CHAPTER TWENTY-THREE

Arthur Brians had fingered his two mates from the night before, so Wilson told us, but he'd like us to take a look at some pictures anyway. If we picked out the two faces, it meant that Arthur would be off the hook with his associates, and perhaps supply the police with further information in his efforts to save his own neck.

The two heavies we'd filled in were called Billy Clarke and Freddy Thomson, and when we pointed them out to Wilson he didn't seem the least bit surprised. They were known associates of Arthur Brians, and predictably they'd vanished off the scene. But Wilson was confident that it was only a matter of time before his men picked them up.

He took statements from Leprechaun and me, telling us that the three faces, all of them having track records for everything from petty theft to bank robbery and grievous bodily harm, would be charged as soon as they were apprehended. He also said that Arthur was happy to stay inside, that he wasn't screaming about his rights, which would have been par for the course, and that he seemed to be scared about being released.

'So whatever it is he's involved in, he's out of his league. But, he's not coughing any more at present.'

It struck me that Wilson had told us more than was necessary, but having developed a certain amount of respect for the guy in the last few days, I didn't think this was any kind of accident.

'Any news from your friend O'Boyle?'

'Are you still saying you're going to charge him?' I asked, trying to avoid giving him a straight answer.

'You haven't answered my question,' Wilson said.

'Look, Inspector.' The Lep came to my rescue. 'We'd be on his side no matter what he'd done, so knowing he's done nothing, you don't think we'd tell you even if we had seen him, do you?'

'It could help him if he'd get in touch.'

'Can I ask you, Inspector?' I looked Wilson straight in the eye. 'How do you know, what makes you so sure Paddy was at the scene of some of the bombings?'

Wilson reflected on the question for a few seconds. 'Information,' he said.

'Is there such a thing as a reliable informant? I mean, could you trust such a man?'

Wilson didn't even have to think about this one. 'Of course not. But you don't look for character references. And we couldn't function without information.'

'So it wouldn't be too hard for someone to drop somebody in it?'

Wilson reacted to this, as though it hadn't occurred to him. He cocked his head slightly then and said. 'You mean someone who had it in for your mate, that they could have dropped information to someone, a known informant, deliberately putting your mate on the spot, that it?'

I nodded. 'Why not? I mean, right now, Paddy is in trouble with you. At least until you decide he's in the clear.'

He sucked on that one for a few seconds. 'It's not a bad theory, but I have two independent witnesses and their descriptions of your mate tally with the stuff we got from the informant.'

The Lep stood up. Can we go now, Inspector?'

Wilson nodded. 'I'll be in touch. You're still staying at Mr O'Reilly's flat?'

Leprechaun grinned. 'Love it, don't I? Wall to wall carpet, hot and cold running pussy. I don't ever want to leave.'

Wilson flashed one of his rare smiles. 'Yes, you chaps do

all right in that department. Quite famous among your work-mates. Or is it infamous?'

'Depends on how old the chicks are,' the Lep answered as we moved to the door.

With a final word about getting in touch with him if we heard from Lautrec, Inspector Wilson watched the Lep take the cab away.

We decided to stop and have a cup of coffee in the Kings Road, just so that we could check if Wilson had anybody following us. In my experience the coffee on that plastic strip of street is crap, but it was worth suffering the taste and the prices, to make sure we were on our own.

'Any idea where we go from here?' The Lep looked at me over his coffee cup.

I pulled my eyes away from the waitress who was a stunning chick altogether. Some kind of Indian or Pakistani, with sensational nut-brown, almond-shaped eyes, and a pair of legs that seemed to go on upwards, all the way to her lovely little boobs.

'And stop piking the waitress. We haven't time for you to be pulling chicks at lunchtime.' He grinned and put his coffee cup down.

'You agree then that we don't just leave things to Wilson?'

'Right, we can't just sit there, hiding Paddy away, hoping the fuzz will come up with the answers. Whoever these geezers are, they've used our mate, they've given him a hard time, and they've put him right in the shit. I say we have to do some-thing about that.'

I nodded. 'You know how I feel about being used.'

Which he did, only too well. It was one of my big hang-ups, especially after the Cecil Davenport business, in which a Home Office guy called Dave Oliver had set me up in the worst way. I hated the idea that there were people with the power to manipulate less fortunate people, to move them about like pieces on a chess board, pull a string and watch them dance like puppets.

'I suppose our best bet, our only bet, is to try that face in Swiss Cottage, the fella who pulled Lautrec on the boat back from Europe.'

Leprechaun nodded. 'According to Paddy, he's the top banana. Heavy too, so we'll have to tread softly.'

I grinned. 'Yeh, they'll all heavy till you start mowing them down.'

'I know I'm not too bright,' the Lep said. 'But I would have thought I'd have worked out what's happening by this stage.' He shook his head. 'I can't figure it out at all.'

'Supposing you were top man in the IRA, here in the Smoke. You'd know you could hire faces like Arthur and his mates, they'll do anything for money, right?'

Leprechaun nodded, and I went on slowly, trying to keep it simple, despite my feeling that the whole situation was too complicated for words.

'You wouldn't really have to tell them too much about what you were doing. You tell them to do something and they do it, provided the readies are there. You get them to plant bombs here and there. And you set up someone like Lautrec, you lean on him in some way, don't ask me how, but something stronger than his story about abortion. You're putting him on the spot so that when you really need to give the law a face, he's elected. And because he's basically harmless, you keep the heat off your own people. Like nobody in his right mind would believe Paddy was in the IRA.'

'Two days ago I'd have laughed at that,' the Lep said seriously. 'But after what happened last night, those faces coming to find us in the boozer. They must have people working for them all over County Kilburn.'

'Right,' I said. 'And we might have been kicked to death last night, you do realise that?'

He nodded. 'Sure. Those pigs'd have no conscience about kicking your head in while you were on the floor.'

'So as you say, we have to tread carefully. They must be on to very big readies if they're prepared to kill. I mean those bombs have killed people and they could have killed a lot more. So what's one more, you or me, to people like that?'

'Let's get back to the pad, see if we can get any more out of Paddy.'

We left the coffee bar and I clocked a fella who looked like a copper. He was standing looking in a window across the street. And he had no trouble at all in seeing us in the backing mirror to the window display.

The Lep and I walked around the corner and when he took the cab away, I saw the fella wave to somebody as he reached the street corner. I smiled, wondering if Wilson wanted us to know he had a man on our tail. If he did, it was all right, if he didn't, the guy on the job was making a complete balls of things.

We got back to Redburn Street just after one o'clock and I saw a car pull up some way down the street. There wasn't a thing we could do about it for now, so I didn't say anything to the Lep. We went indoors and I was relieved to find Lautrec still stretched out on the couch. I moved down the passage to take a leak when the bathroom door opened and my flatmate Annie threw herself at me, and hugged me hard enough to give me a slipped disc.

CHAPTER TWENTY-FOUR

Annie was whimpering beautiful words of relief as I held her to me there in the passage outside the bathroom. Behind us in the living room, I could hear the Lep giving Lautrec a shake to try and wake him up. My flatmate wouldn't let go of me, not that I was in any hurry for that to happen. But I was responding to the nearness of her in the only way I knew how, and she was bound to be noticing my hard on.

She'd bought the newspaper on the way home, and reading Gregory David's article about me and the shooting, well, it had brought it all back to her, and she'd worked herself into a right old state on the ride in from the airport.

'Oh Danny, the thought of anything happening to you. I'd, my God, I think I'd kill myself. You mean so much, so much more than I ever realised.'

I pulled her head back so that I could look at her lovely face. 'Here now, come on, nothing's going to happen to me. I'm the all time survivor, remember?'

She shook her head, her dark eyes brimfilled with tears. 'It's people like you that get hurt, get killed. My God, I thought the trip into town would last forever and then, when I got in, and you weren't here, I thought . . .'

Annie stopped speaking, looking at me like she'd never done before, and I saw her eyes sort of change gear. It was strange, like I had the feeling she was seeing me as I really was, for the very first time. Then her mouth was on mine, her lips yielded to me, her tongue seeking mine, and there was no doubt that this was the prelude to something else.

I heard the Lep give a startled grunt, so at a guess he saw what was happening, but there wasn't a thing I could do to stop it. Not that I wanted to call a halt. I needed Annie at

123

that moment, more than I think I ever needed a woman, and when she pulled her mouth back away from mine, no dialogue was needed to establish what came next. She took my hand and I let her lead me into her room. I kicked the door shut and slipped the bolt. Not that I expected any interruptions, but I wanted her to know that what was going to happen was strictly between us.

Her eyes never left my face as we undressed, then she was drawing me down with her on to the bed, and we were making love, urgently and violently, neither of us concerned about performance or any of that shit. Just burning it up together, needing to burst all over each other, and it wouldn't have mattered if it had taken three minutes or three hours.

I've made love to a lot of women, more than my fair share, I'd say, but all in all, I don't suppose I really remember what it was like with more than about six or seven of them. Like sure, I remember going to bed with a certain chick, and that she was some performer, but I couldn't describe the sensations I knew while we were making love. Like, it's all covered when you say, she was a great lay, or she certainly could throw leg, or whatever. But with Annie, I knew moments that were so special, that I expect to be able to taste them when I'm an old goat with every part of me stiffening up except my cock a doodle dandy.

I was so aware of her that my heart seemed to be pumping at three times its normal speed, just to handle the sensations that were being showered on me. Annie's body met me in more places than I'd ever been aware of before in my life. Her breasts weren't just being flattened by the weight of my chest, they were hard against me, the nipples touching me like fingertips, and the insides of her thighs weren't just holding me tightly, they seemed to be melting into my skin, nourishing every tissue they touched, caressing me and brutally crashing against me, all at the same time.

Inside herself she enveloped me, somehow wrapping me

up, so that I didn't feel I was moving in and out of her. It was more like Annie was holding me in a slender, fur-lined tube, where pinpoints of need and desire and warmth and love pricked my nerve ends until she released me for a second or two, enfolding me tightly again, each time increasing the pressure until I thought my head was going to just take off on me and go crashing up and out through the ceiling.

My dimensions in the genital area are average but she made me feel like a huge rocket, and when I orgasmed, the noises in my head were not too far behind the ones you hear when a spacecraft takes off from Cape Kennedy. I know it sounds too good to be true, but that's what Annie did to me that first time, and I was so spaced that I couldn't even guess at how good it might have been for her. But later, as she lay there, shining, her mouth a permanent smile, I knew that she'd been very close beside me when I crashlanded on the moon.

I lay there smoking a cigarette, watching her drift off to sleep, and when she was sound, I crept out and took a quick shower. The Lep had coffee going and I drank two cups before I said anything to him.

'She was worried about me. I never expected that to happen.'

He smiled. 'You earned it, Irish, and by the looks of you, it was worth waiting for.'

'Too much,' I said, with all the respect I could get into my voice. Like I didn't want him thinking Annie was just another lay because she'd always been more to me than that.

'Just put us in when you can,' he said in his matter of fact way, his blond head shaking as he said, 'They come and they go but you really are the greatest. You sit there, just layin' back, and somehow you get something out of a chick that none of the rest of us do.' He shrugged with his face. 'I don't know how you do it, but you cop more out of sex than I do. Maybe you love them all when you're giving them one,

I dunno, but whatever it is you touched for inside with Annie, I wish I could have a taste of it.'

I didn't say anything because I didn't know what to say. And Lautrec was finally beginning to stir on the couch. He came awake like a puppy dog that hasn't been too well. An eye opened as though it wasn't sure it should bother, then Lautrec let go a sigh of relief as he took in his surroundings. He sat up, his eyes blinking a bit, and he nodded thanks as the Lep carefully pushed a mug of coffee into his hands.

'Get that into you, as the vicar said to the choirboy.'

Lautrec sipped the coffee. Leprechaun and I sat there, watching him like a couple of mother hens, waiting to see that he was all right, trying to judge how long we'd have to wait before we could begin looking for more information from him.

It was good to see that he wasn't shaking, that he didn't need any kind of fix, but I could see he'd be a little while getting it together, so I went into the bathroom again and took a wet shave.

I was in a curious state of mind, and I guessed that I'd done the one thing I'd sworn not to do, which was fall in love with my flatmate, Annie Raglan.

Annie Raglan. I said the name to myself, a few times, watching my mouth in the mirror as it formed the words. Her name wasn't just a series of sounds leaving my mouth but soft palpable shapes that made me think of small brown furry animals, and I was saying it again and again, laughing to myself, tickled at the discovery that I wasn't past taking a chance again.

I was feeling good by the time I sat down to a snack lunch with my two mates, and I was glad to see that Lautrec was looking alive and well.

I left it to Leprechaun to open the batting and I watched Lautrec as he heard about our intention to go after the faces who'd made so much trouble for all of us.

'Like that Arthur taking a shot at Danny the other night. What good is it nobbling him when the face who gave the orders is still walking about, maybe handing the same instructions out to some other git.'

'Thanks a box,' I said to the Lep, hoping that by being lighthearted about the possibility of getting shot at again, I might help Lautrec open up a little bit more than he'd done up to now.

'I wish you'd just forget the whole thing,' Lautrec said after a time.

'Forget it?' I could hear the surprise in my own voice.

'They really are some team. Ruthless, believe me, and I wouldn't give you a snow job. Take my word, stay out of it.'

'We're not going to do that, Paddy. With or without you, we're having a go at these pricks. Just be easier if you'd hit us with some gen, that's all.'

'I'm hitting you with the best dialogue I have. I don't want to see either of you getting shot. I swear to you, this team won't let you get in their way. I know.'

Lautrec was pleading, his eyes burning with the need to be believed.

'We need your help, Paddy, but we'll go without it, if we have to.'

'Fuck you,' he said, sort of choking on his helplessness. 'Is there no way to get you to listen?'

'No way,' the Lep said. 'So come on, Paddy, start coughing and let's see if we can get these geezers off everybody's back.'

CHAPTER TWENTY-FIVE

'I found out that Cornwall's real name is Philip MacLeod. His flat is a really high class drum. Number One A, Appleview.' This was a new block near the top of Fitzjohns Avenue.

Lautrec started slowly, doling out the information with a certain amount of reluctance. But I didn't care whether he wanted to do it or not, and I could see that the Lep felt the same way.

'He's got bread, a lot. Only have to see the pad to realise this. And he gives off that vibe people do when they've never been poor, never known what it is to be insecure about readies.'

Leprechaun said, 'Does he have heavies around the pad?'

Lautrec shook his head. 'Rarely. He has some other gaff where they meet, but they will go to Appleview in an emergency. I know that because it happened one day just after we got back from Europe. I was muffing Penny and he was piking when the face, I think it was that Freddy, arrived. MacLeod wasn't pleased, but it was all right because Freddy had something very important to tell him.'

'What's he got on you? Really, I mean. That abortion story, forget it.'

I tried to sound easy, matter-or-fact, speaking in a flat voice. Wanting him to understand that mate or not, he owed us the truth. Lautrec looked a bit surprised.

'Don't ask me that, please, Head.'

Leprechaun snorted impatiently. 'For fack's sake, Paddy, stop playing about. What difference?'

Lautrec looked hunted suddenly, and I thought he was going to clam up but he said. 'All right. What difference?

They got me to stay as long as they did because they threatened to shoot one of you two, or both of you, if they had to.'

The Lep and I must have mirrored each other's surprise, and it was some seconds before he said. 'Jesus Christ! Talk about scumbags.'

'What could I do?' Lautrec shuddered. 'I talked so much about you pair, wanting to work you both into the scene with Penny. In a matter of days they knew there wasn't anybody else meant anything to me. And they used it. By Christ, did they ever use it?'

'That was how they got you to be there just before the bombs went off?'

'How else?' Lautrec seemed puzzled that I had to ask. 'They could have cut my hampton off and I'd have pissed in their eyes, but I couldn't . . .' His voice trailed off.

'So that was why they shot at the cab.'

He nodded. 'Arthur wasn't trying to hit you. Cornwall, MacLeod told him where to find you. Told him to go close but not to hit you. He didn't want to kill you unless he had to. I'd been getting really stroppy, kidding them that I thought they were putting me on. It was to show me that if I didn't play ball, they'd put a bullet into you and Leprechaun without turning a hair.'

'And you still think we should let them away with all this?' The Lep was seething as he asked Paddy the question.

'Not to just let them off. Because they're too heavy, we couldn't handle them, no way.' Lautrec really believed that, and from the way he spoke, I didn't doubt him for one second.

'Well fack it! I say we go after them. They got no right to do what they did to you . . . I could shoot that geezer, whatsis name, Cornwall, with impunity.'

I knew the Lep well enough to know he wasn't kidding, and

I felt a twitch in my bowels that reminded me how scared I was about the whole scene ahead of us.

'What about you, Irish Danny? What do you say we should do?'

'I think we have to do what we can to put them out of commission. As you say, they can't get away with what they did to Paddy. And fuck it, they're not going to get away with it. We go after them before they take pot shots at us again.'

'I still think you should try and forget the whole thing.' Lautrec was concerned that we were going to come unstuck in the worst way.

'Nah.' The Lep was pacing about he was so pissed off. 'They got to be shown. Can't treat people like they treated you. Then start taking shots at him, just to keep you from getting any ideas that you're a free person. What a fucking liberty! I say we go all the way.'

'There's something else.' Lautrec was reluctant to go on but he obviously hoped that whatever he was about to say, would get the Lep and me to change our minds about doing anything.

'They've got something big to do this week. Bombs. I don't know where and I don't know who they're after. But sometime this week somebody's going to end up in little pieces. Now there's no way they're going to let you two get in the way of that. They'll kill you, don't you understand?'

'And you've no idea where this bombing is going to happen?'

Lautrec shook his head and I believed him but the Lep didn't buy it that easily. 'You sure, Paddy? I mean, you spoofed us a couple of times already. Why not one more time?'

'It's the truth,' Lautrec said, hurt that we were still doubting him.

'Well, try and understand,' I said. 'We don't want to doubt you, but as he says, you did give us some flannel already.'

'Yeh, I know. It's just that I didn't want you to know it was because of you two that I was in bother.' He smiled. 'You might think I was queer for you.'

Leprechaun snorted, mincing a bit like an old queen. 'You're not bright enough to be queer, dear, although I have met one of two Irish poofs in my time.'

We laughed. Relief flowing between us now that things were a bit more out in the open. But still this slight doubt lingering. Was Lautrec laying it on us in all honesty?

He seemed to sense it because he told us again. 'I don't know when or where or why. Or who they're after.'

'Right,' the Lep said. 'Now we got to work out just how we get the ball rolling.'

'We could just knock at the door and push our way in on MacLeod,' I said, not feeling very bright.

'Come on,' the Lep said derisively. 'That's my form but I expect better'n that from you.'

There was silence for about a minute and then I said, 'There's only one way that we can find out where the next bombs go off.'

Lautrec looked up and I watched him as realisation hit him. He nodded, smiling then, accepting what I had in mind before I'd even mentioned it.

'Well tell us what you mean for fack's sake. We're not mind readers.'

I smiled at the Lep. 'Paddy'll tell you. He knows what I mean.'

'Don't mind me,' Leprechaun said.

'I have to go back, don't I?' Lautrec looked at me.

'You don't have to do anything. But that's the one sure way to find out.'

'Nah, you can't ask him to go back to that mob.' Leprechaun dismissed the very idea.

'I'm not asking him to do anything,' I said defensively, feeling guilty that this wasn't the truth. 'But we might just be able to stop whatever it is, if we knew what they're up to.'

'How could I go back?' Lautrec was asking with real interest, which suggested he wasn't against the idea, provided we could come up with a good story.

'Well. Arthur's off the scene, happy to be in custody with Wilson. He told us that this morning. You could blame him. Say he told you to piss off, that he'd be in touch. That he'd call you at Leprechaun's number.'

'How would he have known that, the number?'

'When he told you to get out of the flat, he made it clear you weren't off the hook. That if you pissed him about he'd make sure he didn't miss me next time. So you had no choice but to give him a contact number. And the only one you knew was the Lep's since I'd moved from our old pad.'

Lautrec was looking interested and even the Lep didn't look so unhappy about the idea.

'So, he hasn't called you, and you were worried in case somebody got his wires crossed. You didn't want me getting shot because of some fuck up of Arthur's.'

'Do you think they'd buy that?' Leprechaun asked doubtfully.

'Why not?' I said. 'Look, when we took Arthur away from his mates, they were both unconscious. Supposing he'd just split on them, that he wanted Lautrec out of his pad. Just in case he ended up on a kidnapping charge. Paddy could be forgiven for not arguing with him. But now Paddy's worried, so he goes back. What do you think?'

Lautrec nodded his head. 'I think I can sell them on that.'

'Let's hope so,' the Lep said. 'Otherwise you could cop out real bad.'

'I'll take that chance,' Lautrec said. 'Now let's roll a joint.'

132

CHAPTER TWENTY-SIX

With the decision made, we had a few things to attend to before we could let Lautrec walk back into the lion's den. I got busy on the blower, made a couple of arrangements, and went into the bedroom to wake my lovely Annie.

She woke to my touch and when those dark eyes touched my face, I knew what it was to be loved. I kissed her and it would have been only seconds to lovemaking except I hadn't time for such a luxury.

'I need your help, Annie.'

'And I need to talk to you, very seriously. Suddenly I know I'm in love with you, after all this time.'

I kissed her again. 'We'll talk later, but right now we have to get a move on.'

She nodded but stopped me moving just for another second. 'Is there any chance at all, for us?'

I gave her a grin a mile wide. 'Every chance in the world. Be my girl?' She nodded and I said. 'All right. Now I want you to get yourself together, wear pants. You're going out with Leprechaun.'

She hopped out of bed and my throat went dry at the sight of her lovely body.

'That was Lautrec on the couch sleeping,' I said, and she nodded, smiling.

'I recognised him from his pictures.' Her smile widened. 'But only his face.'

'We've got to get him out of here. There's a copper watching the place. He doesn't know Lautrec is here. So, when you leave here with Leprechaun, I want him to think you're me.'

Annie nodded again, pushing her lovely breasts into her

133

bra, making me wish we were alone in some quiet country hotel, just so I could eat her up.

'So tie up your hair. You can wear that cap you brought me back from the States, my raincoat. If you get into the cab quickly, there's no reason why they shouldn't think you're me.'

She pulled her sweater down over her head and I had second thoughts. 'Can you lose the bra. Those tits'll show up even in my raincoat.'

Annie smiled, delighted with the compliment and I went back into the living room while she pulled the sweater back over her head.

Leprechaun had gone to see a mate of ours, a character who lived on an old tub at the Worlds End. Lonnie Gregson was an electrical engineer with a touch of genius about him. Like he was living gas and electricity free simply because he tapped the necessary sources, and in such a way that nobody had ever found out how he did it.

He made things that were so hot electrically, so advanced that he was now being paid a retainer by a big commercial firm who were keen to market three or four of his inventions. Lonnie didn't care. He wasn't into money or fame. For him the charge was in making the thing, dreaming up a new idea, and I hoped that when the Lep came back, he'd have a bug for Paddy to wear that nobody would tumble to in a hurry.

Lautrec was busy rolling really good joints, using a machine so that they had that tailormade look about them. He was into his second packet by the time I introduced him to Annie, and I knew she didn't mind him boring such a hole in her stash of shit.

Lautrec shook her hand and then he turned to me. 'I thought you told me you didn't have anything going with your lovely flatmate. Can't you see she's crazy about you?'

'I've only just tumbled,' I said, grinning like a fucking idiot.

'You always were a pox bottle.' He grinned and made a sign of the cross. 'I give this union my blessing. For as long as you both shall dig it.'

'How do I look?' Annie had her hair tied up and she had the soft cloth cap she'd given me, jammed on the back of her head.

'That should be fine. Put another sweater on, just in case we're out late.'

She nodded and went into the bedroom. 'Lovely chick,' Lautrec said in a voice free from innuendo. I looked at him in some surprise. I mean, what would have been par for the course was something like 'I'd like to slip her one or two while you're resting up.'

'Even I can change a little bit, Danny,' he said with a grin.

'Don't change too much,' I asked him. 'Like remain one of the survivors.'

He nodded. 'Put money on it.'

The door opened and the Lep came in. He looked pleased. 'That copper didn't know what to do, but he didn't follow me to Lonnie's.'

'Good,' I said. 'Did he have something for you?'

'Take out your earring,' he said to Lautrec.

Without any argument, Paddy unscrewed the ring from his left lobe, and the Lep screwed in a new one that looked to me like a very ordinary earring.

'You are now bugged,' Leprechaun said, producing a small unit like a transistor radio, with a complicated looking dial running the length of it.

'This'll cop a signal up to twenty-five miles even in heavy traffic, so you know we'll be around, all right?'

Lautrec looked relieved and I put my arm about his shoulder. 'You can still pull out of this y'know?'

'I'll be all right. With you two close by, I know I can handle the scene.'

Annie came back to the living room wearing my raincoat.

135

Leprechaun gasped and said. 'What's happened to your Bristols?'

Annie smiled. She liked Leprechaun. 'They're still there.' She blushed suddenly and came to me. I put my arm about her shoulders.

'She's going out of here with you,' I said to the Lep. 'Supposed to be me.'

He nodded. 'Good idea.'

'Thing is, we have to get those fuzz out of the way to get Paddy out of here.'

'What'll you do, take a cab?'

'I thought we'd use your motor. Where is it?'

Leprechaun had to think about that. 'It's in Lillie Road. Parked it there the other night. Before we got involved in this caper. Have a little scrubber up there. Coo. I hope it's still there.'

He threw the keys to me and I put them in my pocket. 'Thank Christ for old Cecil,' I said and he laughed. Cecil Davenport had bought him a car and we'd got a lot of mileage out of wondering what he'd have bought the Lep, if my mate had ever given him a good seeing-to. I mean, he bought him a new family saloon and they'd only ever held hands.

'Go as far as Edgware Road. Into Mifflers for a coffee. I'll meet you there as soon as I've dropped Lautrec at Appleview, all right?'

Leprechaun nodded and looked at Lautrec. 'You sure you can handle this?'

Paddy nodded. 'I'll be all right. It may not show, but my Paddy is up in a big way.'

'Long as it's not your cock, you won't limp anyway.' Leprechaun gave him a hug and jerked his head for Annie to follow him out. She came to me and kissed me, and I held her close for a minute. 'See you in a little while.'

Annie looked up into my eyes. 'Look after yourself.'

136

'I'm good at that,' I said with a grin that was all on top. Inside, I wasn't that sure any more.

She kissed me again. 'That's not all you're good at.'

'Go on,' I said, slapping her arse. 'You'll be getting us all at it.'

She went out after the Lep and I watched the upper half of the cab disappear out of view. That's all you can see from those basement flats. A little while later another car went by but I couldn't see enough of it to know if it was the fuzzmen or not.

'So.' I turned to Lautrec. 'We'd better make a move. If by some chance they haven't gone after the Lep and Annie, we'll just have to lose them.'

He nodded and I put the receiver in my pocket. He fingered the earring and smiled at me. 'First time in my life I was ever happy to be bugged.'

'This is going to work out all right. Believe that.'

'I hope so,' he said carefully. 'Now that I'm switching on to being alive, I wouldn't like anything to happen to it.'

'The second you get an idea of what they're up to, you get out of there. One of us'll be there around the clock.'

He nodded and we moved to the door. 'You can still change your mind,' I said.

'No way, Danny.' He gave me a good hug as though checking I was real. 'Someone has to screw these bastards, and it looks like it's us.'

CHAPTER TWENTY-SEVEN

If the police were still watching the flat I couldn't see them, and I was certain, as we paid off the taxi in Lillie Road, that we hadn't been followed.

The Lep's car, which wasn't actually the one Cecil had bought him, was where he'd left it near Lillie Cross. It was a Triumph Herald he'd bought from a tasty dancer from Streatham or some place, and it was a souped-up motor car because the chick had been into speed.

It started up without any trouble, and I was pleasantly surprised to find more than half a tank of juice. Lautrec sat beside me and I moved off, double checking that there wasn't anybody on our tail.

I drove into Warwick Road, down Holland Road, across the Bush junction and up the new motorway to Marylebone, slipping into Regent's Park, leaving by the top gate. We got to Swiss Cottage and I was still convinced nobody was behind us that shouldn't have been there.

In Fitzjohn's Avenue, I parked a little way down from Appleview, checking that the bug and the receiver worked, which they did. I'd wanted Paddy to see this for his own comfort, but it did me some good too, to hear the bleep the receiver gave off.

'I'll hang on here for a little while,' I told him. 'Make sure you get in all right. And if things don't look good for some reason and you need to split out of there, I'll be here to take you away.'

'Give in about fifteen minutes,' Lautrec said. 'If I haven't come out of there in a hurry by then, it'll be all right.'

'You've memorised my phone number?' He nodded and I said. 'As soon as you get any inkling of what they have in mind, time and place, try and get out of there. Either me or the Lep will be here but naturally we won't be parked right outside the block. Too obvious, all right?'

He nodded. 'Don't worry, I'll find you.'

'The best of luck,' I said, trying not to sound like I felt he was really going to need it.

'I'll see you soon, Danny.' Lautrec didn't look at me as he spoke, then the near side door was slamming shut and I was watching him walk toward the flat block, and I thought he looked very lonely.

I sat in the car smoking a cigarette, and when he hadn't showed at the end of fifteen minutes, I started the motor, and slipped around the one way down towards the Edgware Road.

Annie and Leprechaun were sitting inside the window of Miffler's Café, which ran to a late night delicatessen, and I ordered coffee from a gay waiter who was making a great fuss of the Lep. Annie took my hand under the table and when I saw the relief that flooded her eyes, I knew that my flatmate really had become my girl.

I told them Lautrec was back on the inside and I arranged to take the first shift outside the flat block. It was just after eight o'clock and the Lep agreed to relieve Annie and me by two in the morning. We didn't sit around rapping because we were all tense with concern about Paddy. So we paid the bill, the Lep blew the fairy waiter a wet kiss, which gave the guy a quick flash of the hot flushes, and then Annie and I were driving back up the Edgware Road.

In the café I'd been looking for some sign that Wilson's team had found us, but nobody looking like a flatfoot was paying any attention to us. And as I drove north from Marble Arch, I couldn't see any sign of a car tailing us.

In Fitjohn's Avenue, I parked about twenty yards down from the flatblock, and I was glad I had Annie there with me. 'You think he'll be okay, Danny?'

139

'I have to believe so. I couldn't have let him go back if I didn't think it was going to work out our way.'

'He's a special little guy isn't he?'

I gave her a grin, remembering some of the inspired lunacy that Lautrec had got up to in his time, feeling warm about him simply because he was such a nutter.

'Yeh, he's special all right. Just a pity he had to come back to England involved in something like this. As he said himself, he's sort of climbing back on to the world, but this carry-on could end his hopes before he gets started.'

'Then you do think he's in real danger?'

I turned to look at Annie and I couldn't lie to her. 'I think we all are in a way. But I'd sooner you were with me than not know where you were or what was happening to you. Unless you'd think about going off for a few days.' I had tried to suggest that she nip down to Jamaica, but something had stopped me. Maybe it was because I didn't want her to take any more Magic Banana from those spade guys she'd been into for so long.

'I want to be with you, Danny, if that's what you want.' I nodded and kissed her gently on the mouth. 'I won't ask you to talk about it now, not with all this on your mind.'

'Well, Paddy could get hurt. Like you or me, could have been killed when that Arthur fella blasted out the back window of the cab. But they were setting him up to take a fall anyway. Using the Lep and me as a lever. Threatening us if he didn't do what they wanted.'

'That's monstrous,' Annie said as though she was shivering with cold.

'That's right. These people are fucking monsters, which is why we have to do something about them.'

'Can't the police? Wouldn't they be able to do anything?'

'They're stitched up with red tape. We have nothing to tell them except what Lautrec told us. We even mention his name they'll want to know where he is. The way this guy

140

MacLeod set Paddy up at the scene of some of the bombings, they're not going to fall over believing anything Paddy might say.'

'If they did, couldn't they do something about MacLeod?'

'Annie, listen. Lautrec told us the guy had a lot of bread. Around people with real money the fuzz have to go very easy. If Wilson made a wrong move, he could end up being demoted. No copper's going to risk that for an Irishman called O'Boyle, who's been seen by independent witnesses before some of those recent bombs went off.'

Annie took that in without any trouble. 'So there's no way we can look to the police for help?'

'Not really, and definitely not at the moment. We could probably be nicked for parking here, if they really thumb through the rule book. And if they knew that Lautrec was in there they might go in and nick him. But we'd still know nothing about who these people are planning to blow up.'

'You believe absolutely in Paddy, don't you?'

'Now I do, but for a while he had me and the Lep worried. We knew he was spoofing but then when he told us why, well, it was understandable. Learning that we were the only two people that meant a thing to Lautrec, these Heads used that against him. He didn't want us feeling all guilty about that.'

'And do you think these people are the IRA?'

'I don't know. I want to believe they're not. But Lautrec thinks they might well be. I don't think it makes any difference who they are. We have to do what we can to stop them bombing London. Ordinary English people can't be exposed to this carry on. Life is tough enough for them without them wondering if they're going to be blown to bits, or maimed for life, every time they go out to buy a packet of fags or a loaf of bread.'

'It's horrific when you think of it in those terms.'

'Right,' I said. 'Horrific that people can take the chance of killing other people even, never mind about them going out to deliberately do just that. Christ, it makes your blood go cold.'

Annie cuddled against me and when I kissed her she took my hand and placed it on her breast.

'I love your boobs, Annie.'

'I'm glad, Danny, I want you to love everything about me. If you think you ever can?'

'Oh I don't think that'll be any hardship, loving you,' I grinned. 'I just can't believe the way it happened, that's all.'

'Don't make me ill. God, just thinking that I could have lost you, you could have been killed, before I even realised how much you meant to me.'

'It's all right now. We get this business over and you and I are going off for a few days just to talk.' She looked at me, her eyebrows up somewhere near her hairline.

'And to make love,' I said quickly, before she had a heart attack.

CHAPTER TWENTY-EIGHT

LAUTREC

This is my contribution to the story. From the moment I left Danny sitting in the Lep's Triumph Herald outside Appleview, the flat block where Philip MacLeod had brought me after himself and Penny picked me up on the ferry back from Europe.

Before I go into the details of what happened, I'd just like to make a few remarks about the change in Danny, who, for my apples, was one of the great ravers ever to push a London cab around for a living.

Danny was the most natural puller of birds I'd ever known. Like he had some thing about him that made chicks want to be with him. Not just to get laid by him, but to stick around afterwards as though this time sex had meant something more than it usually did. With the Lep and me it was a bit different. Leprechaun probably got more pussy than any guy I've ever met, but then he worked at it eighteen hours a day, and would dip his wick where angels would fear to tread. Me, I attracted all kinds of tasty and wild nutters, because I was into kinky behaviour as far back as the very early days of my sex life. And for me, group sex was the thing from those early days, because part of my charge was watching what sex did to other people.

Danny used to be into all that, just like the Lep and me, but he'd started to change a while before we lost our licences that time, and then when I met him again after getting back from India, the difference in him was even more marked.

It's like he's growing up a bit, I guess; shame, 'cause he was one of those guys who never should have that happen to him. And it looks like he and this chick Annie have touched for something big. The way she looks at him'd frighten me. I couldn't stand anybody thinking I was that special, well, not for more than a kinky hour or two, anyway.

The Lep hasn't changed at all, looking a bit older maybe, but then he's likely to bounce back and look twenty-eight for another five years, when the dirty basket is more like fifty, at least. Peter Pan in living colour, that's Leprechaun, and he's still as hungry for pussy as ever he was. Like a prick with legs, if you know what I mean. Better off since his old woman left him, I think so anyway. He never could cope with that marriage bit, and even when he knew she was having it away with her boss, he didn't mind. The only time that relationship bothered him was the time his wife and her boss had a row. Christ, the Lep was hopping about like Cupid on a hot plate, trying to patch things up between them. He even offered to give the fella's wife a heavy pull, if her old man would keep on slipping one to his missus. Now, that's what I call heart.

Me? What can I tell you? Something happened to my head after an acid trip that frightened me. I won't go into it. It was just such a bad scene that when I finally touched down, I was so glad to be alive and have some control over my head, that I felt I was walking on water. I'd like to stay alive now, to taste a few of the goodies I never noticed before. I'm talking about simple things that most people take for granted. Toast and marmalade, would you believe? Sitting down to a meal to eat it and not to suffer through it, as I did all my life. Crazy, isn't it? To be thirty-seven years old and feel you're just emerging from the womb. Well, maybe it's picking up the tab for all the time I spent trying to get back into the womb. I don't know.

I do know that I was scared bad as I walked away from Danny and headed for 1A Appleview. But the three of us had agreed we had to do something about MacLeod and his team.

The idea that they could manipulate people, destroy lives, even a life as nothing as mine had been, well, it wasn't on. And if they got away with what they were doing to me, what was to stop them going on, and doing the same thing, maybe worse, to some poor fish who wouldn't even know how to fight back.

It was a bit ironic really, that, having touched for that magic moment when I realised life could be all right, that I should be bogged down in the situation you've been reading about. Still, I tried to boost my ego, maybe it's just a test to see if I'm worth another crack at that one way ride going the wrong way. I hoped that was all it was, a test, and that I came through it, because I'd only recently realised that it wasn't the destination that mattered, not if the journey turned out to be interesting. And I felt it could be as interesting as you wanted to make it. Provided you didn't have a pack of savages like MacLeod and his team, trying to screw your ass without so much as a by-your-leave.

Penny opened the door to me that night and her eyes lit up when she realised it was me. 'Paddy? Come in, baby, come in. . . .' She threw her arms wide, and her great tits shot up even higher.

I stepped into her body, feeling her arms wrap around me as she stashed her lovely tongue in my mouth and practically lifted me off the ground as her hands pulled me by the butt, to get me that much closer to her hot pantied pelvis.

I won't bullshit you that I tried to stay cool, that I was just playing with her to get back on the inside. I'd had enough sex with her to know that she could turn me on if the hangman was about to give me a drop. And things hadn't changed one little bit.

'I've missed your hot cock, baby, missed your tongue, missed your fingers, missed your dialogue desperately.' She was gasping out the phrases, so ready to be screwed that there was no point in keeping her waiting. But I had to ask where MacLeod was?

'Be back in a couple of hours, baby, a couple of hours, oh don't talk, come and give me my friend, come and rifle me, baby, come and give it to me, give it to me good.'

She was backing across the fabulous living room, holding my hands, her blue eyes cloudy as she turned herself on even more. I didn't say a word because she was hitting the right chords for both of us. I mean, if I'd been about to croak, that kind of dialogue would have had me going out the only way a man should. Like, trying to put down a good bunkup just that one more time.

I threw her down on the bed, knowing just what she needed. She played at getting back up, saying no no, as though she was a prim little virgin who would die before she submitted to the soldier with the red helmet. I slapped her on the face and she fell back, covering her face with her hands. I pushed her skirt up on to her stomach, ripping the flimsy little panties she wore. Then, without even taking my clothes off, I produced my hampton, which was burning up to get into Penny's power station.

She moved slightly, her idea of writhing to get out of the way, but it didn't stop me ramming myself into her, and though the breath shot out of her for a second or two, it didn't stop Penny protesting for a few seconds that she was a virgin and that I mustn't, I mustn't. Then she went into part two of her script, the bit where the virgin starts to accept the invader, even begins to like it, then starts to want it, so that when I pretended to take it away from her, she started to thrust upwards to stay on the handle, trying then to pound hard enough for it to pierce her backbone, with Penny throwing in dialogue that would have given an exorcist a tough programme to work on.

Penny was one of the greatest lunatics I'd ever screwed, and without trying to brag, I've had some, in all shapes, sizes

146

and colours. Maybe it had something to do with the fact that she was so hot for me, I mean, ego, we all have, and in the sex area, I've had too many compliments not to have let some of it go to my head, or my cock if you like.

Anyway, not to bore you with the details, I banged her long and good, the way she liked it, and when I finished the steam was gone out of her for a little while.

'I wondered what happened to you, baby. Thought you'd split long gone.'

'It was that Arthur,' I said, rehearsing the dialogue I was going to give MacLeod, if I ever got the chance. I told her about him coming back to his pad alone, releasing me and telling me he'd phone me at my mate's flat. Not hearing from him then, I decided to check things out.

MacLeod sat and listened to the same story, his pale eyes never shifting from me as I talked. He was sitting down so his height wasn't obvious, but when he stood up, his six feet two inch frame looked taller than that because of him being so thin.

As usual he was dressed country style, well, county, anyway. Soft check jacket, cavalry twill pants, well polished brogue shoes, soft shirt and tweed tie. His face was pale as I told him about Arthur, and his long hands clasped each other tightly as I told him that Arthur had warned me not to scarper, and that he'd be in touch in a day or two.

'He said something about the law coming to his place and he didn't want me found there.'

I finished on that, for the moment anyway, and I waited, trying to look and sound like I was puzzled. Penny brought me a drink and pressed one of her boobs against my mouth. MacLeod told her to get away from me, and she did this without any kind of argument.

'I'm surprised you came back.' He spoke with the Oxford accent, his eyes covering me like a camera with double X-ray lenses.

147

'Oh come on,' I said, with a touch of impatience. 'What kept me in the first place is what brought me back. I don't want either of my mates getting shot at, maybe killed. That's all, and you fucking well know it.'

'You were very wise to remember.' He allowed himself the ghost of a smile and said. 'Arthur and his friends seem to have disappeared. I feel sorry for them when they surface again. I don't like people leaving without my permission.'

I said nothing, flipped my tongue at Penny who was lying on a divan, looking as though her pussy was biting the insides of her thighs. MacLeod didn't object and I asked him if it was all right to slip one to Penny. He checked his watch and nodded all right.

'We have time for a little diversion. Suck him first,' he said to Penny, as though he was telling her how much sugar to put in my coffee. Penny started to obey him and I shut my eyes. Might as well grab what's going, I thought.

CHAPTER TWENTY-NINE

LAUTREC

It was uncanny really, the way MacLeod could talk about what was going to happen to Arthur and his mates, then sit and watch Penny give me a blow, his eyes missing nothing. If you'd just walked in and seen him like that, you couldn't but have thought that was all he did to pass the time. Watch other people having it off one way or another, using his money to buy the people concerned.

'Now, put it into her. Hard. Punish her with it, punish Penny.' He was just about yelling and it was no hardship to do what he said.

Penny loved what was happening, getting even more out of sex when MacLeod was there urging the pair of us on. And urge us he did, so much so, that there was no way to drag the sex out, no way to keep it going. It was all too much for the self-control and I exploded into Penny in a matter of minutes.

A while later, when I was dressed and had it all together, I sat on a chair facing MacLeod who was on the couch. I had a drink in my hand and I tried to sound sincere when I said, 'When whatever you have in mind is over, can I stick around?'

He looked at me in some surprise. 'I beg your pardon?'

'What I mean is, I'd like to go on screwing Penny. Maybe I could be your chaffeur or something.'

For a second I thought he was going to laugh but he checked it and pretended to give the suggestion some serious thought. 'We'll see how things go,' he said.

'I could shave off the beard, alter my hair style, and I'd

have no trouble getting a passport in a different name. And you know I can drive anything.'

He nodded. 'Don't bother me with it now. I have things to do that require all the energy I've got.'

'Of course I have thought that maybe you're going to kill me,' I said, as calmly as I could.

He didn't react in any special way. 'That's always a possibility, Declan, but it's not in any way a definite part of my plan.'

'If it's not then, how long before I'll know what you're going to do with me?'

'None of your business but because you're being pretty reasonable, and because you displayed a great deal of common sense in coming back, I'll tell you. My plans during these past few weeks, the indiscriminate bombings, etc. reach their climax tomorrow evening. At exactly nine o'clock.' He stood up like a fella who'd just designed a new way of life for everybody. 'England begins her rise back to the top, to her rightful place amongst the nations of the earth.' He smiled. 'She begins that upward journey soon after nine o'clock tomorrow night.' I nodded, trying to look like I didn't really understand what he was on about. 'You'll let me know when you can after that.'

MacLeod granted me the kind of smile you give to a two-year-old with whom you are determined not to lose your temper.

'I'll let you know.' He checked his watch again. 'Now, I have to go out for a little while. I propose to handcuff you, Declan, just to ensure that you don't undergo any change of heart.' He looked at me and I held out my wrists. I was in now and there was no point in getting stroppy. He took a pair of cuffs from a drawer in his desk and locked them around my wrists.

'Penny will be here to see you don't wander away on us.'

He handed her a revolver complete with silencer. 'If he attempts to leave, shoot him.'

Penny nodded, and I had to wonder what he'd done to her, what he had on her, to make her so sheeplike around him.

He left and I sat down. 'This is ridiculous. I came back, didn't I?'

Penny shrugged helplessly. 'He's funny about some things.'

'That's for sure, and my guess is that he's going to be real funny when he kills me after tomorrow night.'

Penny's face dropped. 'He won't, he couldn't.'

'What's to stop him? He won't need me. He's set me up already. So after the big show, whatever it is tomorrow night, all he has to do is hold me down with the help of his heavies, put a gun in my hand, and help me blow my own brains out. I kill myself and he's free to send me flowers.'

Penny put the gun down and came over to me where I sat. She dropped to her knees, burying her face against my zip. I could feel the heat of her mouth through the material of my trousers.

'He can't, he mustn't. Not you. He can't kill you, kill your lovely cock. He mustn't do that.'

'Take him out,' I said. 'Take him out and let me see you hold him.'

So far so good, I thought. Penny had to know something about what was going to happen. He seemed to discuss everything in front of her, so I'd nothing to lose by seeing how much of her dialogue to me had been real, and how much of it a load of cobblers.

Her hand was like a vice around my hampton, and she put her lips to me. It wasn't easy but I was trying to concentrate on what I had to do. 'Penny, what is he to you?' She didn't stop kissing me but I pressed on. 'Is there a chance that you and me, that we could be together, y'know? Or do you belong to him or something?'

151

Penny's head came up and her blue eyes searched my face. 'What do you mean, you and me? You mean, us, living together or something like that?'

I shrugged. 'Ah, forget it, you probably think I'm just a novelty for a few days. Ugly little guy with a big cock and lots of sexy notions.'

'No you're not,' Penny said angrily. 'You're not just a novelty.'

I grinned. 'Remember what I promised you just before they took me away?'

Her eyes widened and she nodded her head. 'Oh God, do I remember?'

'We'll do it now,' I said. 'But you know it's going to hurt you, probably quite a bit.'

'I want to be hurt like that with you. You know I do. I was practically begging you to dog fashion me. Even though you're so big, I want it, I've got to have it, I don't care if you rip me apart. I've got to know it like that with you, I've got to.'

'You'd better use something, vaseline, something like that.'

She came back from the bathroom, naked, her eyes sparkling in anticipation. I stood up and she took my pants and that off. I really didn't feel all that energetic, but I had the feeling that Penny would be that much more on my side by the time I got through banging her bottom.

She knelt down on the carpet, on all fours and I knelt between her legs.

'I want to live with you Penny. I want to love you, I want my friends, male and female, to love your lovely body.'

'Give it to me, baby. Give it to me now.'

I moved against her, feeling that in all reality, this fuck could mean the difference between life and death for me.

CHAPTER THIRTY

DANNY

A few people went in and a couple of them came out again. That was all that happened in the first few hours that Annie and I were watching Appleview. I didn't recognise anybody but there was a tall thin guy in cavalry twills, the shorty cashmere overcoat, and the curly-brimmed bowler, and he struck me as a possible Cornwall, or to give him his real name, Philip MacLeod.

He came and went in a chauffeur-driven Rolls and even in a high class flat block like that, not too many people owned that kind of car. And Lautrec had laid it on that MacLeod had real money.

What the hell was happening to Paddy? I hoped to Christ they weren't giving him a hard time. Like, there was always the chance they'd laugh at his story. I mean, it wasn't impossible that Arthur Brians could have gotten a message to MacLeod telling him what had happened. If by some chance he'd done that, the team inside number One A Appleview could have been pulling out my mate's toenails by this time.

The thoughts that run through your mind. Maybe that Penny was threatening to castrate him or something. Lautrec had said she did whatever MacLeod ordered her to do, without ever questioning, in any way, his instructions. Jesus, that would be an awful thing to happen to anybody, especially Lautrec though, because he was so into giving pleasure with his jumbo-sized hampton, that he should have been supported by the nation, just to give him more time to share himself around.

Annie was lying against my shoulder, and I ignored my

153

need to be off somewhere with her. Just the two of us. In the country somewhere. Staying at one of those old pub hotels, where you eat what the landlord eats, where they can still be bothered to shove a hot water bottle into your bed at night, and where you can make love to your heart's content, with a good fire burning in the grate. Talk about living, Wow!

Without thinking I flicked on the receiver that Lonnie had supplied to pick up the bugging device Lautrec was wearing in his left ear. Immediately I got a kind of staccato bleep, as though Lautrec was moving with regular movements. Annie looked at me, just as puzzled as I was, then the bleep sound started to speed up, and it got faster and faster and faster.

'What's happening?' Annie had some fear in her curiosity.

'That kinky bastard is getting laid.' I practically choked. 'He's in there laying pipe and I'm sitting out here wondering if he's being tortured.'

The receiver was practically buzzing steadily now and I could just see Paddy as he moved into the vinegar strokes, those last bitter-sweet movements before you pop your cork.

Suddenly the bleeps shuddered to a stop, before the receiver started giving off the kind of occasional bleep you'd expect if the bug was fixed to the ear of a normal guy in a heavy situation. I switched the thing off, picturing Lautrec as he lay on top of the chick, or as he knelt behind her, or whatever, thinking that he was still a beautiful nut. I mean, who else would even think of getting laid in those circumstances?

Feeling a little better, knowing that he wasn't suffering, the cheeky little kink, I found my mind running over one or two moments shared between myself and my two mates. A scene at Lautrec's pad, with Maggie McNab driving a big dyke crazy as she grabbed Paddy by the hampton. I remember the way she jerked it upwards, and I laughed out loud at the memory of Lautrec going up on tiptoe as he tried to move up with her hand and his hampton. How I'd have loved a snapshot of that moment, and the next one too, as Maggie, from a height of about six inches above his policeman's helmet, had poured a glass of beer over Lautrec's big muscle.

Maggie turning to me then, still holding Lautrec's John T. in her left hand.

'You are now looking at the most boring cock I've ever met.' Shaking it then like a dead rat. 'Big and boring, Irish,' she said to me, her voice draped in sincerity. 'You could sit on that and not even notice it.'

I remembered telling her to put him down, that she didn't know where he'd been.

Maggie had nodded agreement to that. 'Isn't that a fact?' she said, her Scottish accent creeping through now. 'The little rat would get up on a tube train.'

While this conversation was taking place, while poor old Lautrec was up and down on his toes like a ballet dancer in training, Leprechaun was giving one to a chick with the ease of a born exhibitionist. And if he was at ease, I had to hand it to the bird he was humping. Like no way was she going to suffer in life on account of being shy.

Bicycle wasn't shy either, but then she was a Duchess, and those chicks are brought up to handle almost any situation. I remembered going to the Mount Regal Hotel in Mayfair, Leprechaun waiting for Lautrec and me to arrive. Warning us to behave as he slipped us fifty quid each, with, he said, more to come.

I was happy to receive that kind of readies, more than a week of nights on the cab, paid in advance, and by all accounts, by a lady who wanted to have a jam session with the three of us. Yet, something had been wrong.

'Wrong?' The Lep had looked puzzled. 'What you on about?'

'It's him,' Lautrec had chimed in, 'the way he's talking.'

'Right,' I'd agreed with Paddy, then to the Lep. 'What's wrong with your mouth?'

Leprechaun grinning. 'Leave off will you. It's the Duchess.

155

Couldn't understand a word I said.' He'd shrugged. 'Anyway, time I started speaking proper.'

Lautrec and I had split a glance, a smile, and a shake of the head that spelled 'total disbelief' in capital letters.

'And no piss taking inside,' the Lep had insisted. 'This is a real lady we got our hands on.'

The Duchess had been standing on her head when we got into the living room after a long walk down a corridor where the carpet ran to near ankle deep. She had very good, long sexy legs, the toes pointing to the ceiling while her skirt sat like a pelmet just above her chin, if you see what I mean. Later on, Lautrec was standing on his head beside her, sharing a joint with the titled raver, his brain practically whirring like a computer as he tried to figure out a way to slip her one while they were both standing upside down.

Annie asked me what I was chuckling about and I told her a few bits and pieces that made her laugh. 'You've really been a crazy bunch, haven't you?' I nodded, grinning at the next memory of Lautrec and she asked me seriously. 'Do you think we can salvage something from it all? I mean, I've been crazy myself for so long. Is there half a chance that we can get enough out of each other to help us start to live half way normal lives?'

'There could be,' I said seriously. 'Just depends on whether we really want it or not. How badly we want what we think we've touched for. It won't just happen.'

'I'd work at it, Danny. I never thought I'd hear myself say it to a man,' she smiled ruefully. 'Or a girl. But I want to live with you, be your mate, if you'll have me. I feel I could love you enough to keep both of us happy enough.'

'Well, Annie, if you think you can live without all that black ham.'

'I've been into black people because they're so natural, Danny. They don't play the games people play to the same degree. Other guys I've had, they're mostly trying to prove

156

how good they are in bed. They need to believe they're the great screws of all time. Blacks aren't like that. They give you what they have to give, they hope it's good for you, but they don't get hung up if it doesn't work.'

'I've always had a soft spot for black chicks myself, but then I've told you that before.'

She smiled. 'I know now why black people would find you so agreeable. You're not one of those guys trying to prove something. You're a giver, you give and give, and they'd love you for that. So do I, and I'm not just talking about bed.'

'I think we're going to make out fine, Annie, and if the odd time you need to go off and freak for a day or two, there's no reason why it should interfere with you and me loving each other.'

She kissed me passionately on the mouth, her hands around my neck and my ears, and I had to make her stop before I started slipping her one in the car. Not that I was against the back seat trick, but I had to keep my mind on Lautrec, even if the dirty little git was getting laid again by this time.

'Oh how I wish this was all over, that we could just be alone for a few days.'

'It'll happen. Be all the better for waiting a few days.'

'I know, Danny.' Her hand found my zip and she started to touch me. I took her hand away. 'Not now, Annie. I want you, but I've got to keep my head. Even though he was screwing that Penny earlier on, Lautrec's still in a very dodgy position.'

CHAPTER THIRTY-ONE

LAUTREC

Penny had me in a dodgy position but I liked it. We were in the bath together, which was no mean trick considering my hands were cuffed together and she was sitting astride me, slipping up and down, on and off my handle, while I tried hard not to drown happily.

It'd taken her twenty minutes or so to recover from that last bang, which had hurt her enough for me to be concerned, while she bucked and yelled about delicious agony, and I hoped that my head wouldn't disintegrate entirely as she drove me on and on with her own special brand of encouragement.

My efforts were paying off, all the same. She'd done some talking while she was relaxing on the bed after she'd staggered away from where I'd knelt behind her on the living room carpet. I'd gone after her, lying beside her then, giving her the kind of dialogue, the after words, as Danny called them, which he claimed were very important to chicks, whether they were virgins or old boilers who had enough cock to make a handrail from Land's End to London.

Penny had appreciated the attention, whether she was aware of it or not. And I'd probed gently, not being too direct in the way I questioned her. And she had let it come out, slowly like someone high on good shit.

'Philip wants Wilson and those other fellows, the Common Market Clan, he calls them. He wants them all out of it, and he means permanently. If he succeeds, he has enough people behind him to bring down the Government and get the Tories back in . . . He wants England to stay out of Europe.

Anybody who wants in is a Communist in his eyes. And with the meeting being televised tomorrow night, he wants the whole country to see Wilson and the rest of them get blown to pieces.'

I lay there no longer able to appreciate the curve of her lovely buttocks. I could hardly believe what I was hearing, but she was so matter-of-fact about it all, that not only was she not spoofing me, she didn't even seem to care about the implications of what MacLeod intended to do the next night at nine o'clock.

'And he's going to lay the blame on the IRA. Very clever.' I tried to sound like I was full of admiration. I didn't want to make even the slightest discord around Penny. I'm not sure she was really aware of what she was telling me, but now that I had her going, I wanted to find out all I could. As soon as I thought I'd heard it all, I'd be up and away, handcuffs or not.

'Philip believes that the country is ready to believe anything about the IRA. Add to the reality of their image, he says. They're in such bad odour, people will believe anything about them, if you present it in the right way.'

'Some trick to get that bomb to go off with all the security they'll have in that place tomorrow night.'

Penny pushed her buttocks backwards to rest against my crotch and I moved a little bit against her. I wanted her to know she could have me again, yet I didn't want her getting too turned on too quickly. She sighed and squirmed a bit more and she felt my hampton twitch. This drew further sighs and more movement from her lovely butt and before I could do anything about it, I was as stretchy as a tom cat lying in the sun.

She decided she wanted to have a bath with me, so that she could sit on and watch my eyes while she went to work on me. The prospect didn't distress me in any way but I'd

159

rather have cooled it until I found out how that bomb was going to be set off.

Penny was giving me more of her fantastic dialogue but any reaction she was getting was a real performance on my part. Like much as I liked what she was doing to the beautiful banana, my mind was on that bomb and the way it was going to be exploded.

'I'm going to go off like a bomb myself,' I said as though I was shouting a warning. 'Careful, Penny, you're likely to get lifted out of the bath.'

'Like a bomb, yes baby, go off like a bomb inside Penny.'

'You should be doing this to that bomb tomorrow night, that'd make it go off. Wow!'

'Radio waves better, means I don't come and go at the same time, ending up in a million pieces.' She was laughing, gurgling in her throat, moving upwards in her head, reaching out for a climax.

'Will you be there, Penny baby? When they press the button? Think of me won't you, think of my cock right up inside you, going off like a bomb inside you, as they press the button. Will you be able to think of that if you're there?'

Her eyes were closed and she was practically swooning but she nodded her head, her mouth hanging open as she gasped in lungfuls of air.

'I'll be there, baby, and I'll think of you, of your lovely dick, as Philip presses the button. When he does, I'll come too, just thinking of you. You'll bring me off by remote control just like the bomb. Oh baby baby baby, now, give it to me now, hard baby hard, yes yes yes, baby . . .' She stopped murmuring the warm words as she touched for her orgasm, her voice choking off as though she was being garrotted, and I let myself go then, heaving for a little while longer until she drew me off, leaving me floundering in the fucking bath, pints of soapy water making me cough like a fella on his last legs.

It took Penny about fifteen minutes to dry me off because every time she gave my hampton a rub with the towel she had to stop and caress him, talk to him as though she expected an answer, and then give him another kiss. All of which could have got me at it again if I hadn't needed badly to get out of there and tell Danny what the score was.

What we did after that, I just didn't know. If I got out of there, I suppose the only thing we could do was go to the law. Danny could tell the story to that guy Wilson, maybe get him to believe it, maybe not. But the law had nothing to lose by checking the scene out, that's if they weren't too busy giving out parking tickets and nicking unfortunate brass nails who were just trying to earn a living.

Penny made us both a drink and she helped me climb back into my knickers. I sat down facing her, marvelling at how she could look so young and innocent, her blue eyes looking as though they'd been well scrubbed and then hung out to dry in a clean ocean breeze.

'Did you mean what you said? About you and me getting it together?'

'What do you think, Penny?'

'I don't know, Paddy,' she said sincerely. 'I'd like to think you meant what you said, but I know what men can be like when they're randy.'

'Well you just sit there,' I said. 'Don't move, and don't come near me or touch me. That way there's a chance I won't get horny for the next five minutes.'

This made her laugh and I tried to ignore her brown legs and the fact that her mini skirt was up around her blouse. Funny that, but no matter how much pipe you lay on a chick, a few minutes later she can look sexier than ever when she's all dressed up again. And this was happening with me and Penny right there in MacLeod's apartment. But I wanted her on my side and I had to impress on her that I was serious about us getting it together. Which, the more I thought about it, wasn't a bad idea. I mean, even though she might fancy me strongly, there'd be no trouble at all attached to getting her involved in good scenes with my mates and that.

'I wouldn't want you to think I'd expect you to have just me,' I said, feeling sure this would appeal to her. 'Like the way you and I are, I'd love to see you perform with my mates, if you'd like that.'

Penny's eyes opened wide. 'Oh baby, I'd love it, just as long as you and I were at it together. I just know we could be happy.'

'There you go,' I said. 'Talking my language. So, how do I get out of here? How do I split and take you with me?'

Penny pursed her mouth for a second, then she said. 'We'd have to kill Philip to have any kind of peace.' I must have reacted very strongly because she went on to say. 'I know that probably surprises you, but he'd never let me go, love. I'm the one thing he owns he can trust. Until now. Now, I'd kill him myself if it meant I could walk out of here with you.'

'That won't be necessary,' I said. 'Just let's you and I split out of here right now.'

Penny nodded. 'All right, but I'm serious about him. He'll have to die before we'll ever be free.' I kissed her and her arms went about my neck. Warm hands in the soft skin of my neck, but they didn't stop me going cold when I heard MacLeod come in, closing the door behind himself.

CHAPTER THIRTY-TWO

LEPRECHAUN

I got very pissed off about eleven o'clock. Trying to work with Lautrec on my mind was no go. For all I knew the poor little git was getting the shit kicked out of him by MacLeod's heavies.

About ten I got a tasty chick into the cab, a big one with auburn hair and eyes to match. She was about five ten, very much my weight, and her bristols were out of sight. I don't mean you couldn't see them, mate, what I mean is, they were so fantastic, they were something else, get me?

Anyway, she tells me Chepstow Road, and I know I'm on a dead pull. I can tell, but don't ask me how. Maybe because of how she looks at me. Not just telling the cabbie where to take her but talking to me like I'm a right fella, that she'd like to know an awful lot better.

Then when I move off, we're in Kensington Church Street, and I'm glad she won't be in the cab too long. Like, I've kinda promised Danny boy I won't be pulling chicks till this business with Lautrec is out of the way. But I know that if I was taking this chick as far as say, Camden Town, I'd be chatting her up by the time I hit Avenue Road.

She parks her lovely bum on the dickey seat behind my head like, and I can nearly taste her perfume. Nice looking bint too, with a big mouth and those heavy lips I love to chew on. With that wet look lipstick that's a turn on even when it's still in the tube.

'Busy tonight, cabbie?' She talks easily, nice accent but not posh.

163

'Mickey Mouse,' I say. 'One of those nights I should've gone drinking.'

She laughs, like someone tickling her fancy, and I'm trying to keep my mind on the road. But it's hard when I consider that those bristols are now pressing against the partition at my back, as she sits half twisted around so that she's talking to my right ear.

Suddenly I know that unless I turn her off real fast, I'm going to try and give her a strong pull. So I wait to see what she says next, and then I'm going to lay it on her that she'll want to get out of the cab right away.

'You could still take the rest of the night off,' she says brightly.

'I could if I had a nice pair of bristols to rest my weary head on,' I say as though I'm telling her the ducks in Regents Park are not too good to eat.

'Bristols?' She says, and for a second I have to ponder whether she's taking the piss or not. Like she seems like she's been around, but that doesn't mean she had to have a smattering of the Ben Lang.

'Bristol City, titty, in the plural titties, boobs, breasts, knockers, whatever you like to call them.'

She doesn't say one word and I think, good. That's shut you up, stop you making my trousers tight. Giving me chat and me trying to be a bleedin' good boy.

I've turned into Pembridge Road when she speaks again. Asking me if I'll stop the cab for just a minute. I do and she asks me something which I can't hear but I turn around to see what she wants.

Well, let me tell you, I nearly fell straight out of the cab. She's sitting there, with her long auburn hair draped over her shoulders. The shoulders are bare and so are the most fantastic set of headlamps I've ever seen.

'Will my bristols do for you to lay your weary head on, cabbie?'

She laughed then, that tickly laugh I'd heard earlier, and I could only guess what my boat race looked like.

'Oh sweetheart,' I said. 'They'll do just lovely. Now what's that address again?'

She told me and I parked the cab just off Chepstow Road in St Stephens Gardens. She has her raincoat on again but she ain't bothered to get back into her blouse or her bra, which ain't bothering me none. Like, she ain't going to be up the stairs and she's going to be out of them real fast.

'What's your name?' she asks me as she closes her flat door behind us.

'Jimmy,' I say, waiting for her to get the raincoat off again.

'My name's Julie.' She takes off the coat and stands there looking at me for a few seconds.

I take her in my arms and she comes into me like I'm a magnet. She's really hungry for some lovin' this Julie and it takes real willpower to let her go long enough for her to get out of her skirt. She takes off her panties then but I stop her doing anything about the suspender belt. Like that's the icing on the cake, as far as I'm concerned.

'Nice to see a girl wearing stockings,' I say, my voice sounding like someone hasn't finished filing the rough edges off it.

'They turn me on. Make me feel sexy.'

She moves over to the divan and I lay down on top of the covers with her. I'm out of my gear by this time, and she can see that she won't have to work at turning me on.

'I love having sex with complete strangers,' she tells me as I lie into her on the divan. 'Gives sex that much more excitement, don't you think?'

'I'll talk to you about it later,' I tell her, slipping her one gently, watching her eyes as she feels me move into her.

'That feels good, Jimmy, very good.' Her eyes are opening and closing, and I start to move very gently in and out of her. She responds quickly and begins to move with me, and in no time flat, I've forgotten Lautrec and Danny, and all I know is that when it comes to dying, I'd like to go out in the arms of a big gentle savage chick like that Julie.

When I finally leave her flat it's half past twelve and I feel like I've done a crash course in square bashing. That Julie's hauled my rocks so hard I'm feeling neutered, but the memory of it all is sitting on my mind like a smile. And I wonder how long it's going to be before I'm back knocking at her door with my henry in my hand.

I'm tired now, but I make a genuine effort to work the cab. Ridiculous, but I'm feeling a bit guilty, see. Like what's Lautrec going through? And what about Danny sitting watching the flats? I mean, I know that Danny, and there's no way he's going to be slipping one to Annie, not when he's got something important to do like be ready should Lautrec need to get away from MacLeod and his team in a hurry.

There's nights you go out on a cab with a hard on choking you and you couldn't pull an apple off a tree. Most nights ain't like that, like you can nearly always bank on one pull a night. Provided you only pick up chicks of course, which is something Danny and Lautrec and I agreed on, once the time hits ten o'clock.

If you're into pulling birds, there's no point in picking up geezers, is there? So, many's the time I've passed fellas standing in the rain screeching for a cab, to stop forty yards on for a chick. All right, it don't do much for your earnings but as I said, you get a lot of snatch.

This night, now that I'm feeling right guilty, I'm willing to pick up a geezer or two. Sort of a penance, know what I mean. But what happens? Nothing but chicks hailing me, and at least two of them looking for a rub of somebody's relic.

One old girl, coughing and spluttering when I first pick her up, starts giving me dialogue right away. Oh, I know you think I'm kidding myself, but I'm not in any need of applause, like it had nothing to do with me.

'My old man used to say I was the sweetest poke he ever had,' this old trout tells me like an advert for herself.

'That must have been nice for 'im,' I say, not wishing to be impolite like.

'On account of me bein' so small down there. Like a school-girl, he used to say.'

'How did he know about schoolgirls then?' I laughed, try-ing to get her mind off her idea about me giving her one.

'Oh he loved schoolgirls did my Harry. Had some too in his time, but he got greedy see. Couldn't just be happy with seventeen-year-olds, even though I let him bring them home an' all. Started to lust after the younger ones as he got older. That's what finished him really.'

'How do you mean?' I ask her, wondering if he had died on the job.

'Well, got him a lot of porridge, didn't it? Man his age going into the Scrubs for a long stretch. Couldn't take it could he? Tried to go queer. Told me himself he made a really genuine effort with the poofs in the nick, but it just wasn't Harry, was it? So one morning he hanged hisself, died he did. Couldn't live without pussy see. Too much man for his own good was Harry.'

'Better off,' I say, meaning it. 'Like, if he couldn't live without pussy, and he couldn't develop a taste for prison pastry, he might as well have topped himself.'

'Yeh, I suppose,' the old girl tells me. 'Only thing is, I have to go out looking for a bitta dick, and when you get to my age it ain't always easy to get one that's got some bone in it. Know what I mean?'

I nodded my head, beginning to feel sorry for the poor old dog. I mean, she was showing a lot of mileage, but it wasn't right that she should be out nearly begging for a stiff uppercut. I didn't say anything though, because I was busy trying to stop myself feeling sorry for her.

'Don't suppose you'd have time to come in and give me a seeing-to, would you?'

I didn't answer her and she said, 'No, well, it's all right. Nice looking man like you, don't need an old pigeon like me. Didn't mind me asking though, son?'

'No, 'course not,' I said, feeling like a right shit.

'You'd be good in the pit, I can tell that. Sexy bastard you are, I know it by talking to you. Still, can't say I blame you, even if I have got a tiny little puss puss.'

Well, what can you do? Leave a poor old trout to another night of loneliness, or do the decent thing and slip her one. I know I'm too soft-hearted for me own good, but I couldn't leave her to an empty room. So I went in and give her a good reading and when I left, I knew I was going to have to spoof Danny about working like a pig on the cab. I mean, much as he liked me, he wasn't likely to think I was a hero, when he was sweating bricks over Lautrec.

CHAPTER THIRTY-THREE

DANNY

I saw the tall slim man return to Appleview, and again I had the feeling that he was the guy Lautrec had talked about.

When he went inside, the Rolls pulled into a parking bay and the chauffeur went into the building as well. I told Annie to sit still and I nipped up along the footpath, moving as quietly as I could. Through the glass doors I saw the chauffeur entering a door to the left of the entrance. When it shut behind him, I crept into the hall area and saw that the number was 1A. So, I'd been right. The tall face was the man of the moment, Mister Philip MacLeod, alias Cornwall.

I walked back to the car and told Annie the news. Not that it changed anything for the moment, but it might come in handy later on. If he didn't know who I was or what I looked like, me knowing him gave me an advantage. Then I remembered the article Gregory David had written in the paper, so I forgot that one. Still, it was good to know what the bastard looked like.

The chauffeur had looked like a tough egg and again I found myself hoping that Lautrec was all right. Which would do my little mate a hell of a lot of good if those faces started to give him a hard time. Still, at that moment, all I could do was hope.

Leprechaun arrived just before two o'clock. He looked tired and I guessed he'd had a hard night on the cab.

'Murder,' he said, touching Annie's cheek affectionately. 'Bleedin' traffic was like on days. Not kiddin', I'm jacked.'

'Do you think you'll be able to stay till eight? I mean, I'll carry on here if you'll take Annie home for me.'

'No way,' he said adamantly, and I felt quite proud of him. He wanted to do his share about Lautrec even if he had worked himself to a standstill on the cab.

'Well, if you're sure,' I said.

'It's all right, I'll stay awake. Don't worry.'

'There's hope for you yet,' I laughed. 'How many nights now since you put one down?'

'Do me favours. Like who needs reminding?'

'I'll see you at eight o'clock.'

He nodded and I gave him the car keys. He handed me the keys to the cab and by the time I pulled away he was already in behind the steering wheel of the Triumph.

Annie sat in the luggage section and her hand on my knee as we drove home was a good feeling. There wasn't much traffic about and we hit Redburn Street without incident. But we weren't indoors ten minutes, like Annie was getting us some supper when the doorbell rang. Not wishing to stick my neck out, I took a peek through the curtains. Wilson was standing there with a copper I hadn't seen before. I went and opened the door and I knew right away that Wilson wasn't in the best of humour.

'All right, Mister O'Reilly. What's your little game?'

He stood facing me, while the other cop hung around near the door. Annie came from the kitchen with a couple of cold plates and some coffee. Wilson didn't speak to her and I sat down beside her on the couch.

'Do you mind if I eat my supper while we talk, Inspector. I'm starved.'

Wilson seemed about to object but he nodded all right. 'I don't know what's up your nose, but I'm prepared to wait till you feel like telling me,' I said.

'You gave some of my men the run around earlier tonight. And I want to know where you've been since then?'

'Your men?' I asked, putting on my incredulous face.

'Christ! We thought they were part of the team that shot at Annie and me the other night.'

He didn't like that but he couldn't just dismiss it. Not with the way I was acting, he couldn't. 'Where's your friend O'Connor?'

'He's with a chick somewhere. I'm not sure who she is so I don't know the address.' I ate another piece of chicken. 'Would you like some coffee?'

He nodded and I looked at Annie. She didn't speak but she came back from the kitchen with two drinking mugs and Wilson and his mate had a coffee each.

'Are you interested in a little idle hypothesis now that you're here?' I asked Wilson, killing a mouthful of food.

'Just as long as you don't get smart,' he smiled. 'I was just beginning to like you.'

'Supposing I told you that tomorrow or the next day, or very shortly afterwards, the people who've been planting those bombs around the place, that they planned another job, only this time, with a difference.' He didn't say a word so I carried on. 'Supposing I told you that they plan a bombing that will really be the final move, after this phoney build up they've been going through. What would you say to that?'

'I'd say tell me more.' He smiled again. 'I might even say please.'

'Suppose I told you that my mate, Lautrec, known to you as Declan O'Boyle, was set up to be at the scene of those bombings, that he was going to be the fall guy, what would you say to that?'

'That I'd like to hear this from Mister O'Boyle,' Wilson said.

'You can't, Inspector, because he's gone back to the team you really want.'

'Gone back? You mean he got free of his obligations to them.' He smiled. 'Now if that was true, why on earth would an innocent man go back to them?'

'Do you know how they got him to do what they wanted? They threatened to shoot either me or Leprechaun, that's Jimmy O'Connor. Or even both of us, if he wouldn't play ball.'

'So that shooting the other night was for his benefit?'

'That's right. Arthur Brians did that, didn't matter to him whether he killed me or not. He might even have killed Annie, but that wouldn't have bothered him either.'

'And you're telling me, hypothetically of course, that your friend O'Boyle went back?'

'We decided that your hands are tied with red tape. That you need more evidence than we can possibly provide before you can make a move. So we've made our own move, and Paddy's back in there trying to get the word as to how and when. As soon as we know, we'll tell you, in the hope that we'll have enough to get you to move.'

Wilson seemed to be sifting this through his filter-tipped mind. I ate some more of my food. Finally he said, 'If I take a chance on you lot, what guarantee have I that you'll come to me when you know what's going on? How do I know you won't just take the law into your own hands?'

'We're just cab drivers, Inspector. We don't want any bother. This business had been thrust upon us. As soon as we can get out from under, you have my word we'll do it.'

'You know where these people are, right now?'

I nodded. 'Leprechaun and I are covering them in shifts. He's on duty till eight o'clock.'

'I want to know where they are, and I want to know now.'

'I can't tell you that. If you go in there now before we know exactly what they're going to do, Paddy could end up doing time for something he'd never done, and the face responsible will get off scot free because he's got a whole bundle of money.'

'You're convinced that your friend O'Boyle is totally innocent?' Wilson seemed very impressed.

'I know it. Look, there must be someone in your life that you can trust completely. Everybody has someone like that. Well, I have Leprechaun and Lautrec, and Annie here.'

'There's no way I can force you to tell me. I mean, this is all hypothetical, anyway, right?'

I smiled, letting him see that I was really grateful. 'Yeh, but as soon as it looks like becoming even remotely real, I'll be on to you like a flash.'

'You'd better be, otherwise it won't be just your friend O'Boyle who could be in trouble.'

'Will you give us a break. Don't move till I give you the word. We have to nail these people to get Paddy off the hook they've got him on.'

Wilson nodded. 'It's on your own head. Don't come crying to me if they decide to dispense with O'Boyle before you get to them.'

'Thanks, Inspector,' I said. 'That's really going to help me get a few hour's sleep.'

CHAPTER THIRTY-FOUR

LAUTREC

After MacLeod came back and the chauffeur, a heavy pig named Johnnie Johns came into the pad, MacLeod told Penny to go to bed. I was still handcuffed but he handed Johnnie the revolver and told him to keep an eye on me.

'There's been a slight change of plan, Declan, but nothing to concern you.' He smiled. 'England will be on the way up about ten hours earlier than I'd expected. All to the good, what.'

He followed Penny into their bedroom and I watched big Johnnie make himself comfortable in a chair facing me. I was tired after all that screwing with Penny, but I wasn't in any way sleepy. You'd have to put in a lot of practice to get sleepy when a guy is holding a loaded revolver on you.

Johnnie didn't talk to me, but then he didn't really talk to anyone. A pig to look at and a pig in every other department too. I closed my eyes, wishing that I could go to sleep but whenever I took a peep through barely opened lids, Johnnie the pig was sitting like a tired totem pole.

Penny had given me all I needed to get out of there. But there was no way, not with Johnnie and that gun. So I tried to sleep even a little bit, knowing that I was going to need all the energy I could muster, if I was going to come out of this scene alive. Like, I knew now that MacLeod had no intention of keeping me alive after the deal he planned tomorrow. Maybe Penny believed he wouldn't kill me, but it was more wishful thinking on her part than anything else.

Harold Wilson and all those other faces were going on television for the first time tomorrow. To discuss Britain and the Common Market on television, so that the ordinary punter could know exactly what was going on. And MacLeod saw this as his opportunity to rid the country of a whole lot of people his kind didn't approve of, plus a fair smattering of Continental top men, all seeking, so he claimed, to bring Great Britain from her knees right down on her face.

Through me, well through my dead body, after he made it look like I'd blown the top off my tiny pointed head, he hoped to put it all on the IRA. With a name like mine, even those cats would have a job getting anybody to believe I had nothing to do with them. In fact, people would be only too chuffed to believe that they were responsible, their image having taken a real beating in the last few years.

All I had to do to avoid being killed and used as a scapegoat, was to get away from Johnnie the pig, and that couldn't be any more difficult than crashing alone through the Brigade of Guards.

He was dozing was Johnnie, by about three in the morning, but not enough for me to take a chance on slipping past him. Being handcuffed didn't do much for the self-confidence, and I wasn't in the market for a bullet up the cobblers, not yet, anyway.

Now, I've always been pretty pleased with my hampton. I mean, it's given me a lot of fun in its time, and without waving the flag, I like to think it's passed on a few good waves to a chick or two along the way. But when Penny crept out of MacLeod's bedroom, I knew that between my dialogue about the future, and the way I'd given her the magic banana, she was really and truly on my side. And when she hit Johnnie over the head with an electric iron, I'd have given my hampton a rub of congratulations, except that such a gesture was likely to turn Penny on and have her begging for a length before we even managed to get out of the gaff.

Johnnie released a sigh like a pig with a hangover, and he would have fallen down on the carpet but for Penny holding

175

him into the chair until I got to him and moved him a bit so that he remained seated, however unconsciously he did it.

Penny unlocked the handcuffs, and while I rubbed my wrists, she picked up the gun. When she turned to face me the light from the standard lamp featured her breasts, braless under her tight sweater, and I had to shake my head not to jump on her there and then. Relief, gratitude, lust, affection, caring for her, call it what you like, I wanted to make love to that chick more than you'd believe.

She put her hand to her lips and made a move for the bedroom. I stopped her, my hand on her arm.

'Let's get out of here,' I whispered.

'I've got to kill him first. We'll never have any peace unless I do.'

I realised she was deadly serious, but I shook my head and relieved her of the gun. Jesus Christ! I was facing all kinds of numbers when it came to years in the nick. All I needed was an accessary to murder charge as well to give me a full house with all the chimneys stacked.

'That'll be my job,' I said, thinking of Danny and the way he gave chicks the Bogey shit from time to time. 'When the time is right.' I kissed her on the mouth.

'Come on,' I said then. 'We have a lot to do.'

She came with me, her eyes wide at my cool, with me glad the light was soft. Like there was no way she could tell by my face just how scared I was.

Leprechaun saw me at the same time I saw him. He sat still and I drew Penny along behind me, close to the wall, wanting to be as close to the car as possible before I brought her with me across the road.

The Lep started the engine as Penny tumbled into the back seat with me lurching in on top of her. She pulled my mouth to hers as Leprechaun let out the clutch and then her arms were about my neck, and I surrendered from sheer relief.

'Coo! Don't you never think of nothing else?' the Lep

moaned towards the rear view mirror, and I untangled my-self from Penny, and sat up.

'This is Penny. Penny this is Leprechaun.'

'Pleased to meet you, darlin',' he said, then to me. 'Where we going?'

'Down to Danny's pad, nice and easy. We don't want to get nicked for speeding, I've got a shooter here.'

Leprechaun laughed and I knew he was relieved too. 'By the looks of your lovely mate there, you'd better slip it into her holster.'

Penny smiled and pulled me against her. The heat of her body, despite the March morning, was like a suction pump and I didn't pull against it. Why should I? She'd just helped me get a reprieve from the wooden overcoat scene, and apart from wanting her anyway, I owed her some show of gratitude.

Lautrec had to sit and wait a few minutes outside the pad in Redburn Street, like there was no way Penny and I could get up until the job was finished. Penny was making a lot of noise, and the Lep had turned to watch us at this stage, and I could feel the extra charge she got from him being there.

When I came, I touched her off at the same time, and she shuddered against me, driving the Lep crazy with her closing dialogue. I turned and gave him a grin.

'You go and knock Danny up while we get the knickers back on, all right, love?'

He nodded, his mouth tight, like he was experiencing the pangs of deprivation.

'Some chick, I'll tell you that, you little pox bottle.'

Then he was gone and Penny was telling me she loved me, that she'd do anything just to live with me.

'Wait till we get this scene over and I'll never give you time to even try on a new dress,' I whispered, avoiding her kiss of delight.

Danny was too sleepy to take anything in until we'd dropped a couple of coffees each. Then I told him everything, except the name of the place where the televised discussion was coming from. I didn't know where, so I couldn't fill him in on that.

'It's Westminster Hall,' Penny said. Danny looked up as though he was seeing her for the first time.

'You're welcome aboard, Penny. And if this bastard ever gives you a hard time you just tell me and I'll pull the cork out of his head, all right.' He smiled and she looked warm.

'He hard times me the way I like it, if you see what I mean,' Penny said.

Danny grinned at myself and the Lep. 'I can guess what you mean, Penny. Anyway, you're sure it's Westminster Hall?'

Penny nodded. 'I heard Philip talking to some guy on the phone. He mentioned that name.'

'Come breakfast,' Danny said. 'And we'll get Wilson in on this, all right?'

I must have looked uncertain because he said then. 'Don't worry, Head, Wilson's turned out okay and we'll do a deal before we give him anything.'

I looked at the Lep and he confirmed this with a nod of his blond head. 'I think I'll kip for an hour or two.'

Danny said, 'I don't think so. If MacLeod discovers Lautrec and Penny have scarpered, he might just come here with a team. We wouldn't want to be caught in the sack.'

'You're right,' the Lep said, 'I hate you but you're right.'

CHAPTER THIRTY-FIVE

DANNY

I took the gun from Lautrec and made him go take a bath. Penny insisted on going with him, which was all right by me, but the Lep sat there green with envy.

'See the form on her. Coo! Unbelievable.'

'Come on,' I said, grinning. 'You've had dozens that good in your time.'

I poured some more coffee and considered waking Annie. But I decided to leave her for a while longer. No point in breaking her sleep before I had to do it.

By eight o'clock we'd all freshened up and Annie was putting her make-up together in the bathroom. We were both tired after more lovemaking than was good sense under the circumstances. But the adrenalin had started to flow well from the moment I'd opened the door to Leprechaun, and I knew I'd get through the day without too much pain.

'You, me and Penny,' I said to the Lep. 'We'll go see Wilson and tell him the story. Lautrec and Annie can poodle behind us, staying out of sight while we talk to Wilson. That way we'll be close enough to look after each other, but he won't be able to nobble Paddy, all right?'

Leprechaun nodded his approval and I told Lautrec when he came out of my bedroom. He wasn't that keen to be out of the front line but he saw the sense of what I had in mind and he agreed to go along with it. He knew I wanted Wilson to get his hands on MacLeod and his faces, and that this was our chief bargaining wedge when it came to talking about what happened to Paddy.

Wilson listened to the story from me, then he heard Penny's side of it.

'What's your relationship with Philip MacLeod?' Wilson asked her.

'He's my father,' Penny said, in a matter-of-fact voice.

I tried not to let my astonishment show. After what Lautrec had told the Lep and me about MacLeod getting his charge watching Penny get screwed, it wasn't easy, and I have to hand it to the Lep for the way he controlled everything except his eyes.

'Paddy stopped me from killing him this morning. In his sleep. He should die, he's so evil,' Penny said and I really wondered what shape the inside of her head was in. She was talking like it was about knitting or something.

'We'll get statements down on paper later on,' Wilson said. 'So none of this is for the record.' He was looking at me and I knew he was telling me to get Penny to keep that bit to herself when it came to statement time.

'Now I've got some calls to make. If there are bombs in the Westminster Hall we'll find them. Meanwhile, I'll go and pick up Mister MacLeod.' He looked at Penny. 'Your testimony will do the trick, especially when we catch him with the contraption for sending the radio waves necessary to explode the bombs.'

A copper came in with coffee for all of us and Wilson got busy on the phone. When he finished he said. 'We'll know within thirty minutes about the bombs. We might as well wait for the news before we pick up MacLeod.'

He stood up. 'I'll go and organise someone to take a statement from Miss MacLeod.'

When he left I marked Penny's card about offering snippets of information like the bit about her intention to kill her big bad daddy. She smiled and nodded her head. I wasn't sure how seriously she took me, so I laid it on her about being with Paddy, which she wouldn't be if she was locked up

180

in a psychiatric unit. That got through and I relaxed as she started to give her statement to a uniformed copper.

Wilson came off the phone after his chat with the bomb people and he didn't look at all pleased.

'There are no bombs in the Westminster Hall,' he said, his eyes flat. 'So who's kidding who?'

I looked from Wilson to Penny. She was just wrapping up her statement. The copper left to have it typed up and I watched Penny as Wilson repeated the dialogue about no bombs.

'He's into a new way of using plastic. Not great lumps of it that anyone looking would find easily.' She was really trying to think about it. 'I heard him say something once. About lino tiles covering a multitude.'

'Lino tiles?' Wilson knew she wasn't kidding and so did I. But it still sounded a little screwy to both of us.

'Could they have the bombs under the floor? What're these geezers doing? Are they sitting on some kind of platform?'

We all looked at Leprechaun and I was thrilled with the bastard. He kept on surprising you like that, coming in with a good one out of the blue, when it often appeared that he wasn't even listening to what was being said.

Wilson killed my enthusiasm by saying. 'The disposal boys examined the raised platform on which the Prime Minister and the others will be sitting. They say it's clean.'

'You mean they didn't find any bombs as such,' I said. 'But if he's into some new way of using plastic like Penny's said, maybe they missed whatever it is.'

It was close to ten o'clock, so whatever was to be found, we had only two hours in which to find it.

Wilson looked at me. 'I'd like you there, all three of you, when I pick up MacLeod. Somehow we've got to pressure him into telling us how those bombs have been planted.'

'I'm glad about one thing,' I said. 'You are talking about

181

bombs. You're not wondering about whether they're there or not.'

He nodded. 'I know they are. This young lady has convinced me of that much. Now let's go.'

I asked Wilson if the Lep and Penny could travel in the cab with me. He said all right and took off in a police car with two plain clothes men, apart from the uniformed driver.

I thought a bit about Wilson as I followed the police car through the park. He was giving us a real break. . . . Taking us on trust, and I only hoped things worked out good for him. So many coppers would have had to go somewhere else to get a decision about what to do, and in our situation, you couldn't have blamed them.

Lautrec was behind with Annie beside him and I was glad Wilson didn't know they were there. I mean, he was being good to us, he was more than all right for a copper, but if he saw Lautrec he just might react like a copper and nick him.

I wasn't surprised that MacLeod wasn't at home when we got there. The minute he realised Penny was gone, he was bound to split. Even if he thought I'd whacked Johnnie the pig with the iron, and kidnapped Penny, he still wouldn't take the chance of being caught at home. She might just talk, and he wouldn't allow a small thing like that to stop him at the last fence. But where the hell was he? That's what I wanted to know.

'We'll go down to the Westminster Hall. Take a look for ourselves.'

I said all right and moved off behind the police car. Lautrec pulled away from the kerb behind me, and I used the cab to block any chance the driver might have of seeing my tail from the police car. He probably wouldn't have noticed in a million years but as I've told you before, I can be bloody dramatic when the mood takes me.

The security was tight at Westminster Hall but Wilson was known to the faces in charge and we soon had the run of the place. The platform was up on the stage. Television cameras were already in position, and there were crews organising themselves all over the place. Nobody paid any attention as we moved the chairs and tables from the raised platform. This was bolted to the floor of the stage and we undid the slip bolts. Then the Lep and I, helped Wilson and his boys turn over the platform unit which was in two sections.

I'd noticed that the surface had been tiled with black and white lino squares, but the underneath was clean of any obvious bomb. There wasn't a nut out of place under there. I thought the main section, the under part of the surface, looked a bit thick, like more than the depth of a wooden plank, or a piece of chipboard, but I guessed the people who were going to be on the platform were important enough to warrant maybe an extra plank of wood or two.

Wilson looked at me and I shrugged. 'We've got to find MacLeod,' he said.

'He drives a Rolls, well his chauffeur does. Penny, tell Inspector Wilson the number.'

Penny rattled off the registration number and Wilson sent one of his men out to put out a call over the radio for information about the whereabouts of the car. Then we put the raised platform back in position, fixed the furniture again, and walked down the hall to the front door.

'Where do you think he might be?' I asked Penny.

Penny was nervous, more so than I'd seen her be before. 'I don't know, Danny. He could be anywhere in London.'

'Maybe the bombs haven't arrived yet,' Wilson said like he was thinking out loud.

'They're here all right,' Penny said. 'I know it. And all he has to do is set off a radio wave to blow it up.'

'And you've no idea where your father might be?'

'He has flats in London, places even I don't know about.'

We were still kicking this around when the driver of the

183

police car came to Wilson. 'The Rolls, sir. It's parked in Pimlico. I've got the exact location.'

Wilson looked at me. 'We've nothing to lose. You follow us.'

I jumped behind the wheel of the cab, which was parked near the hot dog stand thanks to Wilson knowing the copper on duty. When I took off after Wilson, I was pleased to see Lautrec and Annie in the Triumph slot in behind me.

There's a joke about a fella going the wrong way down a one way street, and he stopped by a copper who tells him it's a one way street. And the motorist says but I'm only going one way.

The guy who crashed into Wilson's patrol car didn't find out he was going the wrong way until it was much too late, and I had to swerve hard to avoid ending up as part of the pile up. By the time I thought of stopping I was on to the lower end of Buckingham Palace Road, the crash having happened on at the bottom of the triangle that forms Grosvenor Gardens. So I kept on, hoping Wilson was all right, but deciding that we had to be able to find the Rolls.

CHAPTER THIRTY-SIX

It took a quarter of an hour before we touched for the Rolls. It was parked just off Warwick Way and I slipped the cab in between an old van and a truck parked a little way down the street. I wasn't exactly elated. I mean, being that close to the Rolls was one thing, but there were thousands of apartments in that area, so we weren't that much better off.

I climbed into the back of the cab with the Lep and Penny. He was thinking along the same lines as myself.

'You could get lost down here, nobody'd ever find you if you didn't want to be found.'

Penny suddenly realised that we had a problem and again she practically had me falling over when she said, 'Maybe I could talk to Daddy on the phone, find out that way.'

Leprechaun looked at me in disbelief and I smiled by way of reciprocation.

'Talk to Daddy on the phone?'

'Yes,' Penny said as though I was very dumb. 'There's a phone in the car.'

'But the car's bound to be locked up,' the Lep said, beating me to it.

'Oh, I have a key.'

'But you don't know where your father is, so how can you ring him?' I asked, this time feeling really dumb myself.

'I phone his answering service. Surely they'd know where he is. He never does anything without leaving a number.'

'Y'know, you're not just a pretty face, and a fantastic pair of bristols.' The Lep leered at Penny with a new-found respect. 'You think too, you lovely darlin'.'

We kicked the idea around, working out just what Penny should say to MacLeod if she did manage to make contact. Then I left the Lep inside the cab. He was to wait for a signal from me. Penny walked up to the Rolls and let herself into it. She flicked the nearside door open and I crept in as surreptitiously as you can creep into a Rolls.

It took her about a minute to get MacLeod on the line and then she went into the act we'd rehearsed.

'Oh Daddy, Paddy took me with him after he clobbered Johnnie. I only went because he threatened to shoot you as you slept. I got away from him because he fell asleep himself. I was going mad, riding around, not knowing where you were. It was pure chance that I saw the Rolls, oh Daddy, where are you? Let me come to you, please?'

I heard MacLeod's voice crackle at her through the radio phone and then she put the receiver down and turned to me with a smile.

'He's in one eight six,' she said. 'First floor flat.'

I nodded my appreciation of the good news, trying not to let it show that I thought her pretty strange to be selling her father down the river this way, even if he was a technicolor shit.

The Lep arrived beside the car, hunched down beside the nearside door.

'He's in one eight six, first floor,' I said. 'Let Penny head over there. You start now, coming at it from this side. I'm going to nip up the street and walk back down. All right?'

The Lep nodded and moved off as Penny swung her lovely thighs out of the front seat. I scarpered swiftly up the road, stopping about fifteen yards above number one eight six.

Penny was approaching the door now, with the Lep already stashed to one side of the entrance. I started back down, trying to time my arrival at the bottom of the steps with the moment when the door opened.

I could see Penny talking into the safety device and then there was a buzz as the door swung open. The Lep was through behind Penny by the time I got to the top of the steps. I flashed through and allowed the door to swing shut behind me.

Penny started up the stairs and I moved behind her. The

Lep was crouched a bit behind me. The idea was that if someone came to take a look they just might not see us behind Penny, who was sticking her gorgeous tits out so far I thought she'd just tumble over on her face.

The first floor flat door opened and Johnnie the pig managed a startled expression before I hit him across the nose with the gun. He stepped back and I hit him again, throwing the door wide for the Lep to join me.

It was a huge room, and it contained MacLeod sitting in an armchair near the window at one end, and another thug of frightening proportions. Leprechaun barrelled straight into him, and I lost my concentration for a second as I watched him bury his right fist in the thug's heavy chin.

MacLeod sprang up with a gun in his hand. 'Drop it,' he said. 'Or your friend gets it right this second.'

The Lep was just finishing off the big fella who was on his knees on the way to the floor. He turned and saw the gun in MacLeod's hand. His eyes flicked to me telling me not to drop my gun, but I couldn't take the risk of MacLeod shooting him down on the spot.

'I won't tell you again.' MacLeod didn't look like he was kidding and sick as I was, I had to drop the gun.

Penny went into a routine we hadn't worked out. Falling down on her knees, weeping, whimpering like a frightened animal, as she poured out a tale of how we'd threatened to kill her if she didn't do what we said.

MacLeod accepted this like a man who wasn't bothered one way or the other. 'Sit down, gentlemen, and make no mistake, I'm a crack shot.'

The Lep sat down on a chair close to the unconscious thug's body and I slumped onto the divan on my left. Penny was still kneeling. The phone rang and MacLeod lifted it without taking his eyes from any of us.

'Yes. What? Oh well, good, it'll be that much sooner. Thanks.'

He put the phone back on the base and smiled. 'For the first time in the history of public debate, the participants have arrived on time. They'll be seated in exactly five minutes, then, hey presto and we'll be rid of quite a bunch of left wingers.'

His free hand pulled a small unit like a transistor lying on its back that much closer across the table where the phone sat.

'One button, gentlemen, a small amount of pressure with one finger and my task is over for the present.'

'Will you tell me something?' I said. 'How will you do it? I mean, you must know that platform has been checked for bombs.'

He nodded. 'Naturally, Mister O'Toole O'Reilly.' I smiled at his use of my right and proper names.

'The entire floor is plastic. The kind that goes boom when you hit it in the right way with a radio wave. Believe me, when that lot goes off, nobody on that platform is getting away with a broken limb or two.'

'That's diabolical.' The Lep spat the words out.

'Fiendishly clever yes.' MacLeod smiled and I thought of rushing him. One thing was sure, if it was going to be done, it had to be done now.

'We've got to take him, Lep,' I said loudly. 'He can't shoot the two of us at the same time.'

I stood up very slowly, my heart pounding, and I watched the Lep rise at the same pace as myself. I thought I saw MacLeod's finger tighten on the trigger but that could have been imagination. His other hand was very close to the button he intended to press, and I was glued to the spot with a numbing kind of fear.

The shot didn't make much noise. A kind of phut sound, but it sent MacLeod reeling back and away from the table. His gun hand came up and he seemed about to kill at least one of us, then his eyes lost their glow, it was like someone had turned off a light, and he pitched forward on his face, all life gone out of him.

I turned and watched the gun drop from Penny's fingers, saw the flicker of a smile play around the edge of her mouth. 'He was bad, Danny. I had to do it.'

Wilson arrived at this moment, followed by Lautrec and Annie and a couple of his men. He took a quick look around, saw the transmitter on the table and looked back to me.

'The whole floor of that platform is made up of explosive material. All it needs is a touch from that button and we'll need a new Prime Minister.'

'Jesus Christ!' Wilson sounded exhausted. 'He nearly made it.'

'If it hadn't been for Paddy, ehm, Declan O'Boyle here, and Penny, he would have made it. And I'm not kidding or giving you any shit.'

Wilson nodded and shook Paddy by the hand. 'Thanks, Mister O'Boyle. Really glad to meet you.'

He turned to Penny who was ready to climb all over Lautrec. 'What you did, it took a lot of guts, a fair bit of patriotism, to put your country before your own father. That won't be forgotten.'

Annie was leaning against me, and I felt how tired she was. Like me, she needed a good night's sleep.

Wilson picked up the phone and began making all kinds of arrangements.

I asked him if we could go. I said I needed to sleep and he said all right. That he'd be around to see me at about eight that evening. The others trooped out and I moved behind Annie.

Wilson called to me and I turned. He indicated the button on the transmitter.

'I suppose that in time, we may be forgiven for saving Wilson.'

'We're lucky in a way, 'cause so few people are going to know about it, that it can't do us too much harm. See you.'

I left him standing there with a smile on his face.

EPILOGUE

About a week later when everything had been sorted out, like we'd all made out statements and what have you, I started work one evening with a job to the Atheneum Club, which is, as you know, a geriatric clinic posing as a club for elite gentlemen.

I was being paid off by this curly-brimmed bowler when I saw this other fella go into the club. A tall guy with golden hair and long tapering fingers hidden in sheer kid gloves. I had to bite my tongue not to call out after him, for as you might imagine after all that had happened, I was more than surprised to have touched once more for the Paperhanger.

I hopped out of the cab and ran into the club only to be stopped short by a Sergeant Major Shite type, who thought he was still in the army.

'Just a mo, just a mo, where do we think we're running to then?' He had seen my cab badge which, in a place like that, is an invitation to be treated as a fucking imbecile.

'Fella just walked in, golden hair, kid gloves. I want to talk to him.'

'We want to talk to him do we? And what might the gentleman's name to be then, 'Orace?'

'I don't know his name, but you better get him out here or I'm going to start screaming for the law. He bounced a kite on me, a big one.'

The protruding eyes reacted to this in a way that suggested the guy wasn't all that surprised. He fingered his obligatory moustache and said to me with just a touch of something other than derision. 'Just a mo, sir, don't go away.'

'As if I would,' I said, grinning evilly at him.

A fella arrived in a frock coat and striped trousers, nice sort of a man, and no messing about. He drew me to one side of the entrance and asked me what was this about a cheque bouncing. I told him in plain language about the way some-one had been hanging paper on taxi drivers. That I'd seen the guy, the one with the golden hair going into the club.

'That's Lord Plater,' he said, 'and I have to tell you that I'm empowered to pay you the amount due to you. His Lord-ship is a fine man but every so often he takes ehm, little flights of fancy.' He smiled telling me he knew I understood and that he'd appreciate me not broadcasting the news.

'How much did his lordship make the cheque out for?'

'Thirty pounds,' I said, deadpan. 'He was on a shopping spree the day he conned me.'

I deliberately threw in the word about conning me, like this guy had started to react badly to the amount I'd mentioned. 'And I know at least twenty-nine other drivers who've been caught too,' I chipped in for good measure.

'Do you have the cheque?' He wasn't going to be heavy but he had to make a try.

'It's with the police, and maybe that's where I should be right now.'

He peeled off thirty lids from a roll that was in good shape, and then he added an extra fiver. 'For being so understand-ing,' he said.

'Can I tell the other drivers to ask for you?'

He nodded, reluctantly. 'Yes, I suppose you may, Car-ruthers is my name.'

'Thank you, Mister Carruthers,' I said. 'I won't send them all to you on the same night.'

Back in the cab I laughed at my own daring. Stroking an extra score for all the aggravation the Paperhanger had caused me and my mates, chuffed with myself for finding him even if it was accidentally. And I decided to take Leprechaun, Paddy, Penny, some bird called Julie that the Lep was bang-ing, and very tasty too, with Annie and myself when we had our night out the next evening. The thirty-five would go a long way to covering the Darby O'Gill, and so what if we had to have a whip around for the balance, or a tip for the waiter.

I felt good. Annie and I were working out fine with no heavy dialogue about forever and ever. Penny and Lautrec seemed to have something worthwhile going too. The Lep and Julie, I wasn't sure about. She was probably a real nice girl, wanting to settle down, but with him being so into sex with perfect strangers, I didn't think there was much hope of her getting her hands on him for more than a week or two.

Who cares? I mean a week or two that's good, is favourite over those spoken guarantees of a lifetime's loyalty and all that jazz. We were all doing okay at the moment, and that was good. I mean you never know what lies around the corner. You can only hope there's another piece of roadway. Especially when you're driving a London cab.